THE THIRD SISTER

A novel that continues what Jane Austen's *Sense and Sensibility* began!

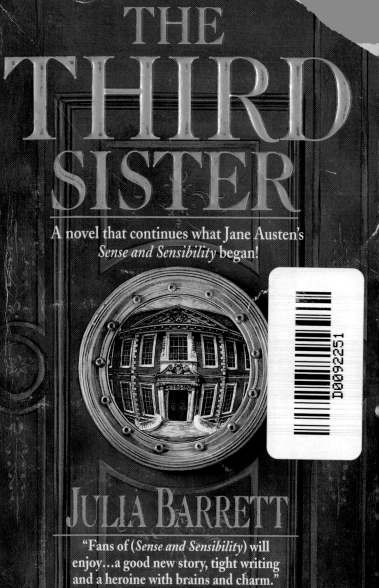

JULIA BARRETT

MIRA™

$5.99 U. S.
$6.99 CAN.

ISBN 1-55166-446-1

9 781551 664460

50599

Praise for Julia Barrett's novel
Presumption,
a sequel to Jane Austen's
Pride and Prejudice

"If you're a Jane Austen fan, you'll be happy to know that a miracle has happened. It's a sequel to *Pride and Prejudice* and it's wonderful...near flawlessly written."
—*Book Page*

"Expertly captures Austen's ironic voice and subject matter in a book that is sure to delight and intrigue Austen devotees."
—*Library Journal*

"An elegant, airy delight."
—*New York Daily News*

"A firm fix on Austen's style and a finely tuned ear for her barbed dialogue...even the persnickety Miss Austen would approve."
—*Chicago Tribune*

"Eminently enjoyable."
—*Los Angeles Times Book Review*

"Energetically and often delightfully handled, evoking the spirit of *Pride and Prejudice*."
—*New York Times Book Review*

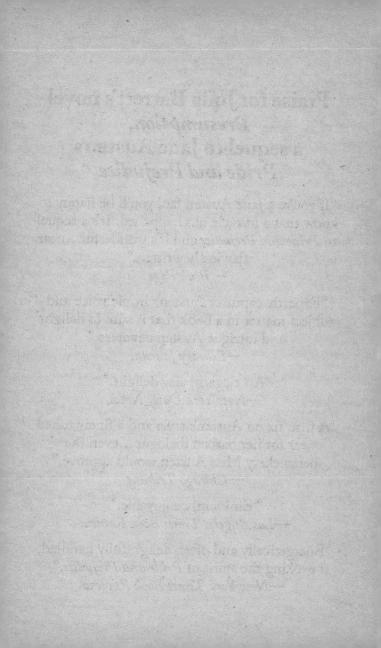

THE
THIRD
SISTER

A Continuation of Jane Austen's
Sense and Sensibility

JULIA BARRETT

MIRA

ISBN 1-55166-446-1

THE THIRD SISTER

Copyright © 1996 by Julia Braun Kessler.

Reprinted by arrangement with Donald I. Fine Books, an imprint of Penguin Books USA Inc.

Margaret, the other sister, was a good-humored well-disposed girl; but as she had already imbibed a good deal of Marianne's romance, without having much of her sense, she did not, at thirteen, bid fair to equal her sisters at a more advanced period of life.

(Chapter 1)

Mrs. Dashwood was prudent enough to remain at the cottage, without attempting a removal to Delaford; and fortunately for Sir John and Mrs. Jennings, when Marianne was taken from them, Margaret had reached an age highly suitable for dancing, and not very ineligible for being supposed to have a lover.

(Conclusion)
—*Sense and Sensibility* by Jane Austen

Part One

1

Sorry is the portion of a third sister. While most concur that in your good family the first child is more properly born male, a cooing, caressable baby who chances instead to be a girl will soon provide sweet recompense for her indecorous choice of gender. The welcome for a second daughter is perhaps less assured: yet, in households where indulgence prevails, she—petted and fretted by not only mother but elder sister too—may find herself to be even more happily situated than a first of her sex. Alas, however, for the careless miss who, lured by this enticing portrait of domestic felicity, elects to follow hard upon.

Such was the imprudence of Margaret Dashwood of Barton Cottage in Devonshire; and how ill this earliest blunder served her! Slighted throughout childhood not only by her sisters, but—oh, the injustice of it—by the Muse herself (a veritabe giant of letters just then loosed upon the world, and that lady who fashioned them all), it fell to her to stand

by, spiritless and dull, as her sisters' characters
were formed and reformed, their loves lost and regained—and all this without so much as a nod in
poor Margaret's direction.

She had been constrained the while to watch her
sensible eldest sister Elinor suffer torments before
her marriage, and those made only the sharper for
being undergone in self-governing silence. She was
next obliged to look on as the more passionate second of her family, Marianne, was encouraged, then
cruelly abandoned by an unthinking villain, John
Willoughby. Margaret had known her beloved sister
nearly to die of a fever, and then to recover only
for marriage with one nearly twice her age, and he,
moreover, given to wearing flannel waistcoats.

Growing up as she had, witness to flaring tem-
pers, to bursting confessions, to disappointments,
miseries, oftentimes coupled with Marianne's trans-
ports of ecstasy—while yet scorned by the One who
might properly be supposed to have known better,
as having imbibed far too much romance while having made little if any sense of it all—it would
hardly have startled if this last Miss Dashwood, as
she was initially delineated, had turned out to be a
creature with wits altogether addled.

To the contrary, by the time she reached her sev-
enteenth year, *our* Margaret Dashwood stood proof
that even Genius might at times be disposed towards too hasty an estimation. Margaret's singularity, when examined, was considerable. Not only
was her judgment precise, her understanding was
swift. She had read as widely as many, and com-

prehended more than most: nor was this learning
achieved at any sacrifice to her sweetness of nature.
Let her word be taken as of little weight, her own
comfort regarded as disposable; her mind and temper persisted, one as good as the other, worthy
enough, in short, to secure for her just tenure as our
heroine.

None had yet descried such potentialities in the
young girl. None save her father, whose passing but
three years earlier she still grieved. Henry Dashwood, of Norland, in Sussex, unlike certain lesser
gentlemen who discover themselves married to
women of meaner intelligence, had maintained a
cheerful household by dwelling rather upon Mrs.
Dashwood's genuine warmth of heart and liveliness
of disposition, than upon the limits of her understanding. He had been laudably devoted to each of
his amiable daughters, and perhaps more com-
mendably still, had held in no less affection his
firstborn, their half-brother John; but it must be acknowledged that in young Margaret he found the
true blessing of his ultimate years.

She alone, free from the too restricted character
of Elinor's temper, and of the too-much openness
of Marianne's, effected to marry the best attributes
of himself and of his wife. As she grew from infancy to girlhood, he began moreover to discern in
her a particularity sadly absent in the rest of his
family—that of an agile wit, complemented by an
evermore deft articulation. Though she spoke
softly, there was laughter in her voice; and with
each year it seemed her perceptions of the foibles

of her near relations became finer, her appreciation of them firmer. His anticipation was keen of that day when, with Margaret full grown, they could indulge in the levity that, for all the satisfactions life had afforded him, had long been lacking. Pity for both, he did not live to see that time.

The shock of his loss at so tender an age for Margaret was soon followed by other vicissitudes, none of them it is true quite so wounding to her heart, but afflicting her sorely nonetheless. Although Mr. Dashwood had sought to secure his family's future, a valuable bequest was not his to bestow. For most of his life, his fortune had depended upon the benevolence of his great-uncle, an old gentleman erratic in his ways. Margaret and her sisters had been early taught to anticipate his every want, to humor each idiosyncrasy, accommodating themselves to silence while he took his daytime rest, and to utter darkness in the evenings, until he deemed that the candles might be lit. Each of the Dashwood children—Margaret in particular—had for their father's sake, and from the goodness of their own warm hearts, attempted all that seemed possible, to comfort their relation in his waning years.

Alas for devotion. Readily did the old gentleman accept their ministrations; yet it was only when their brother, John Dashwood, fully grown and master of an independent fortune, made his appearance at Norland, that their great-uncle truly bestirred himself.

John Dashwood had over his sisters a twofold

advantage: there was first his masculinity of gender, and with it, a means of address so remote as could contrive to distance him from the scene altogether. On his rare visits, after his first greeting he was seldom heard to speak at all. These talents were to serve him better by far than all his family's loving attention.

When as the years progressed, Dashwood added to these attractions first an elegant wife, and then a baby boy, the old man's affection—and, shortly before he died, the greater part of his estate as well—were pledged altogether.

Thus it was, that at Henry Dashwood's untimely decease, which followed not long after, the hopes of all that family were left to the philanthropic proficiency of their brother. His obligations the young man fulfilled with such solicitude that it was scarcely long before Mrs. Dashwood and her daughters found themselves in near poverty, moved from the only house and lands they knew, and cast into exile in a cottage in Devonshire.

Elinor and Marianne, it will be remembered, rose to the challenge and secured their lives, making an excellent account of themselves in fortunate marriages. Thus the financial distress of Mrs. Dashwood and Margaret was somewhat relieved; but that relief came at the cost of increased loneliness. Since, at their departure, her mother required the third sister the more pressingly, such trips as Margaret might have hoped for to her prospering sisters—visits liberally offered by both—were, if not postponed altogether, invariably cut short. Mother and daughter remained much alone at Barton.

But if the pains of seclusion were theirs, the comforts usually attendant upon solitude escaped them. Not half a mile from Barton Cottage stood Barton Park, home of Mrs. Dashwood's kinsmen, Sir John and Lady Middleton. Sir John, whose goodness of heart was equaled only by his want of taste, proved relentless in his efforts to extend hospitality to the forsaken pair; and since his good Lady was by nature and breeding impassive—and too sensible besides of certain interests of her own to nay-say him—many an evening was engaged for them at Barton Park.

Mrs. Dashwood, continuing fond of society and sure of the Barton table, attended such diversions with cheerfulness. But for Margaret there could be no such expectation. Knowing now the country families as she did, she could foresee boredom at best; at worst, exposure to meanness of spirit. Still, to reassure her mother, she affected amusement; although the company and the manner of discourse she sought, she knew was not to be discovered at Barton Park.

Happily none of her listlessness communicated itself to Sir John. *His* pleasure in her companionship was eager, his attentions to her unremitting. He had moreover a design for his young cousin. Always had he delighted in bringing forward within his orbit smart young people to promote alliances. Now, fired by what he confidently appropriated as the reward for his success with the elder Dashwood sisters, whose matches—in fairness to the gentleman—he had not actually impeded, he determined that he should not rest until he had performed a similar service on behalf of the youngest. Let her prefer it or not, he would see her happy.

Little did the good gentleman recognize the strenuousness of the task. For much more woefully than was at the time surmised had Margaret been affected by her sister Marianne's wretched treatment at the hands of Willoughby.

Lady Middleton's own satisfaction in her young visitor equaled her husband's, although it sprang from a less disinterested source. *He* wished only to provide for her the bounty of the wedded estate; *she* saw in Margaret a more material asset: the capability, most wondrous to her, of controlling her children.

It had been three years and many months since the high spirits of her Ladyship's darlings had been admired by one Lucy Steele and her sister; three long years of growing limbs, expanding lungs, and spirits which, entirely unrestrained by any direction, had begun to achieve such a frenzy as even their mother must notice. Far be it for Lady Middleton to be so little tender as to discipline them; yet she had in the interval of their growth been obliged to spend a little time in the company of her angels, and when the untried Miss Dashwood, by firmness of voice and look, achieved calm, the good Lady could not but approve.

Margaret was therefore, as often as not, enlisted to render assistance in the nursery. Since no one,

certainly neither her sadly unimproved mother nor
her absent sisters, saw any better use for her, all
interests were thus most admirably served, if those
of the least important, Margaret herself, were not.

Still, it could not be denied that Lady Middleton's years of maternal experience must needs put
her to educating the novice in the finer points of
governance.

"My dear Miss Dashwood," began she one autumn afternoon, so soon as her voice could be
heard, in that very room, "I must remind you that
children are creatures quite unlike ourselves. You
cannot be too harsh in your eagerness for harmony.
It was but in a spirit of loving brotherhood that John
shook William. Nor can I too often caution you
upon such childish vivacity, which is a fragile virtue, too easily bruised. You see how William stands
on his legs again. What a spirited fellow he is, is
not he? Now, do continue, but pray, speak out more
loudly with your pretty tale, so that we may all hear
it, for Annamaria's bouncing does make such a
noise. She listens sweetly though, does not she?
while her little sister Mary has only been lulled to
sleep. What joy for a mother to see in your lap so
hearty a girl, and she only six! How you are to be
envied," continued she with a sigh, "to profit thus
from the pleasures of our little ones, and still bear
none of the burden. Ah, my dear, were you only
yourself a mother, could you fully understand your
present good fortune."

Margaret, while caressing the child, must marvel
at those mysterious endowments of motherhood

which, as magically as the genie's spell in the story she was telling, made selflessness of self-solicitude, and of obduracy, wisdom.

"What a charming group is here," cried Sir John, just then returning from the sale of a pointer in Exeter, his aspect the more buoyant at the sight of his guest, since he had only just endured a full hour of solitude. "I vow, Miss Margaret," now studying her after having first clasped his young children and wife in greeting, "you do grow more lovely day by day. Your own Mama and I, my love," turning towards Lady Middleton, "were remarking upon it this very morning. It puts us in recollection," with a meaningful gesture, "of a young person who must be invited to Barton Park to agree with us. As good a fellow as ever lived. I cannot imagine how we did not bethink ourselves of him before. He is something silent, to be sure; but no matter, when he ventures to speak a word it is scarcely worth comment. Still, his is a manly look, and an amiable one when it is his day to be so, and mark you, he owns a fine stable in Lincolnshire. Know this much at last—for I'm mindful that young ladies do love a mystery—that his name begins with a P. He arrives on Saturday."

Margaret colored as she sat, too discomfited to attempt response.

Lady Middleton, nothing daunted, merely gazed upon her husband and cried, "Come, my love, what would Miss Dashwood want with beaux? You must pay no heed, my dear, to Sir John, or, to my mother for all that. They *will* tease you with a prospect of

matrimony, a fine estate, new ball gowns and bonnets for the asking; but I shall never be a party to
it. Only *I* am privy to the harsher side of the bargain. Look how cozy you are, right here at home
among us, with our own dear lambs! What situation
could be happier? I assure you, my dear Miss Dashwood," she then added kindly, contriving to lower
her voice to an undertone, "when this young man
appears, we together shall take care that he give you
little bother. You shall wear the green sarcenet I
gave you, since it so little favors your complexion.
And to ensure your safety yet further, you must
look to it you sleep but little on Friday night; certainly you should never smile in his presence. Depend upon it, he will betake himself to Lincolnshire
in no time, and we shall rejoice once more in our
happy circle, secured from interference for as long
as we may choose."

"Your Ladyship's generosity is as bounteous as
I have grown to expect," replied Margaret, smiling
and altogether diverted by her stratagem. "And I
own, that for that particular result, I can conceive
no more effective an abetment than your green
sarcenet."

Her Ladyship nodded satisfaction. The while,
Margaret could but ponder which fate were the
bleaker, extended companionship with the Lady or
with one chosen by her good husband. She was
satisfied to entertain herself by concluding that each
must inflict a torment not to be undone by the other.
It was only later, upon further reflection, that the
meagerness of choice presented by her own circum-

stance in life was brought home to her, and then
alone did it prove enough to try even her philosophical soul.

2

More fortunate during these years was Elinor, the eldest of the Dashwood sisters. Her own marriage and removal from Barton Cottage had proved tonic. It is true that withal she had suffered sore losses. Those bracing intimacies with her far too easily stirred mother; the no less ardent exchanges with her dearest sister, Marianne, who, until too lately could never do *anything* by halves. And during this absence, perforce she could not but abandon the overseeing of all such niceties in Margaret, the still unreclaimed youngest of her family.

Heavy privations indeed. But if pressed, even Elinor must allow that the steadfast presence of her husband was recompense for any such suffering. For in truth, the former Miss Dashwood, in her married state, was finally able to discover what it meant to be herself.

Since the death of their dear father, Elinor had assumed the regulation of her family's appearances before the world. It was she—the eldest daughter vigilant and sensible—who kept rein upon her too precipitate relations, and she alone whose forbearance had quieted their rashest inclinations. Without question, she had been their savior over former years. Her mother and sister now lamented what might have become of them were it not for Elinor's unwavering self-command. But in that purpose, her brow was ever knit and her cautious nature anxious. The reserved Elinor we recognize paid no small price for her good sense.

It was marriage to Edward Ferrars that brought her respite. Was it not he, after all, who had secured for her newer claims, a broader license to life? Between them was easy reliance, each upon the other, and his dependability she found so reassuring that she rejoiced in her deliverance, even, for the very first time in her life, found leave to face fancies of her own.

The pair had indeed taken up living at Delaford in Dorsetshire, promised to them by the Dashwoods' friend, and now Marianne's husband, Colonel Brandon, and this well before he himself had arrived with his own bride at Delaford House. And though Lady Middleton's mother Mrs. Jennings' prior prediction regarding the bleak material prospects for them in the choice of their way of life was not altogether overstatement, the young people's joy in their union was such that little could touch upon its perfect happiness.

Neither Elinor nor Edward could see reason for discontent in their modest circumstances. Mr. Ferrars was a man who plainly preferred the happy contemplation of his wife to the regret of his reduced income. His earnest disposition, his eagerness and dedication, his love of service, and above else, his good fortune in having escaped an earlier and near disastrous attachment, sustained him amply day by day. He saw himself a lucky man altogether.

The Delaford Parsonage in Dorset had now become their home. Those very lodgings which Colonel Brandon had once pronounced comfortable only for a bachelor met their simple needs more aptly than the Colonel could have supposed. And with some few improvements, combined with Elinor's clever management, the house could even be seen, if not ample, as well-appointed. It stood across the lane from the village church, a white-walled building with massive chimney-stacks, spreading roof, and large uncurtained windows to embrace the evening light. There were honeysuckle and clematis that hung about its porch, and at the far end could be seen a brick wall which divided the flower garden in front from the kitchen garden beyond. A long glance across the uneven lawn framed a fine, ancient cedar.

If it was not grand, yet there was harmony in the view and a natural grace at every turn, even when the weeds were given special liberty, and they often were, to flourish equally with the brashest colors of the plantings.

Elinor and Edward, moreover, were able to see their Mother and Margaret, and their other friends welcomed comfortably, if not often, within their home. Always the pair was blessed with good food since their own kitchen garden was deemed worthy of any grander establishment. Along with such bounty, Mr. Ferrars had been industrious in the cultivation of his glebe; his sheep and cattle, grazed and fattened, fed the household adequately.

Nor did their small income prevent the couple from offering Sunday hospitality to those of Mr. Ferrars' congregation who had come to the service from outlying farms. Any might sit down with him and his wife, usually attended by Mr. Barker, the church warden, at the parsonage table to refresh themselves with warm broth and converse before beginning their journey home. Such exchange enabled Mr. Ferrars to keep abreast of circumstances in his parish.

"Surely, Mr. Ferrars," said Mrs. Blythe, a farmer's wife of the county, on one such occasion, "you intend to move swiftly in this insupportable matter of the Haddam boy?"

"Insupportable?" queried Edward. "Young Haddam has never appeared to me but polite and cheerful."

"To the point, sir," replied she. "Why, the boy positively will not leave off. Singing in the church out of turn, drowning out all else. Such antics will bring scandal to the whole neighborhood!"

"My good Mrs. Blythe," said Edward. "Surely, you cannot be serious for one moment together. James is young yet and will frolic. Perhaps he shows in his singing more energy than decorum; but must there then be a remedy for high spirits?''

Mr. Barker, who had acted as churchwarden for over forty years, was obliged by this outlandish sentiment to rush to the defense of propriety. "A church," pronounced he, "is a fit place for worship, not rapture. But," with a meaning glance, "perhaps our new parson is too gentle of birth to trouble himself with such a trifling concern as to discipline his parish?''

These words cut Edward. Like him, there had ever been those of gentle birth in the County who looked to entering the clergy as a comfortable solution for indecision regarding the choice of a profession. The prospect of even the smallest living to be had for the asking could prove the best incentive for such idle young men—a secure path towards respectability. And many another *did* succumb to the temptation. Alas, as Edward had too often observed, they were subsequently seldom seen in their parishes.

Edward Ferrars had come to understand long ago, even during his earliest years as a student, the consequence of such neglect. He had himself seen good, simple Devonshire folk grow indifferent, making scarce so much as an appearance at a Sunday Matins. Too many families had turned their backs upon the English Church altogether, preferring instead the more flamboyant dissenters, and Edward observed this change with sorrow.

In those early years, while he had struggled on his own, confused, without guidance, facing disapproval from his family, he had pondered deeply about his hopes, and determined to remain firm in his duty to his flock.

But he checked himself before continuing. And when he did speak, it was in a playful tone.

"You think me, perhaps, one of the sporting parsons?" said he. "Those clerics who attend more devoutly to the call of the horn than to the lure of the pulpit? I well recall such an one during my student days. A Mr. Dixon, then parson of Modbury— portly, robust, a soul of good cheer. He could game and dance with the best well into the night; and how often would I greet him of a morning on his way to hounds, or carrying his rod, and not a thought in his head but for the sport. I remember in particular," said he with a smile, "a day when the good parson needs must put off a christening. 'Patience, dear madam,' I heard him urge the babe's mother, 'Can't have babies baptized while the font is full of minnows for Monday's angling.'"

Mrs. Ferrars was much diverted by this tale, but Mr. Barker shook his head dolefully and would have none of it.

"Pray forgive my levity, my good sir," said Edward observing the older man's discomfiture. "I perceive that I am in danger of being thought by you as one of those churchmen chastised by Cowper as 'loose in morals, and in manners vain, in conversation frivolous, at once rapacious and profuse.' Yet, be assured, that I, with him, pray for nothing more than that the Church be preserved from such apostles as those!"

Fortunately for the young parson, there were exchanges far more gratifying to him than this one. These were the days he went out about the business of the parish. Easy was he talking to his tradesman, walking about the fields with his farmers, and seeking out those in the service at the manor house, always with an ear for their woes, and a way of smoothing their differences. His direct address and kindly humor soon earned him their confidence, and before long he had brought back to Delaford parish the order and decorum it lacked.

Better still, as the time passed, he rekindled an enthusiasm among his flock for all that he thought to be the good in the tradition of his Church. His most valuable tool in this endeavor was the too often overlooked virtue of Christian charity. There was little of the small-minded or puritanical in Edward Ferrars. His judgments were always exact and fine. Nor could he remain at variance with any good soul about him. And if it might be suggested that his sermons lacked the fire and zeal of the Evangelicals, still the new rector made it up by intelligence, a good heart, and a cheerful disposition to win the love of his parishioners.

To be sure, the parish, like any other, was not without incident. Despite all of Edward's successes in the short time he had been at Delaford, each day brought the young man new vexations.

"This will never do," laughed Elinor one evening, after clasping her weary husband in the warmest greeting. "Can it be that our church musicians are besetting you yet again?"

Poor Edward could but shake his head.

"Never have I seen the like," said he, "they will not hear a word of counsel. Russell has had words with Phillpotts; bassoonist cannot, will not abide the flautist. Why, the two nearly come to blows in the very loft itself. Any listeners would take them for fishmongers, not musicians at all!"

And he fell silent. Much display he could settle; but these ungovernable rages, and from those who could so enchant with the sublime art of music, left him speechless.

Elinor would have laughed heartily over his predicament, so preposterous did it seem, had she not noted the dejection that informed her husband's face. Instead, she sat thoughtful for a short spell while devising a little scheme of her own.

"Artists," said she, "are most commonly of such disposition, dear Mr. Ferrars, depend upon it. Their temperaments are unlike those of the rest of us. You cannot compel them to agree. Still, we needs must have music of a Sunday. I venture to suggest a means of making them, if not precisely biddable, then tolerable at least."

Edward, worn as he was, heard her eagerly.

"How, my love, might they resist an invitation from Mrs. Brandon to play at a ball at Delaford! Marianne's accomplishment in and love of music you well know; and if our good players' skills are not quite as fine as those of the Exeter group she is accustomed to importing, still I'm sure that she will serve us well in this for the occasion. Such an event—an evening at the House in the gracious presence of my sister—I warrant you—will sweeten their temper and make their music, like their dispositions, more harmonious than ever before.''

Her husband smiled in silence. The prospect of his beautiful sister-in-law's quieting his musicians' squabbles was a delight to contemplate.

"My dearest," laughed he, "Colonel and Mrs. Brandon could do no better for the welfare of their parish if they themselves went about the cottages distributing bountiful gifts to the children!''

Both derived from this conversation the most comfortable of feelings; Edward, upon the prospect of peace in the choir loft; Elinor, the sweeter consolation of serving her beleaguered spouse.

3

What then of Marianne, the sister in between, a young lady born to discover at a tender age how her own befuddled romantic fancies could lead her far amiss? Having already taken her place as the lady of Delaford House, *she* had even secured, within her short tenure there, a position as revered patroness of the fair Dorset hamlet adjacent.

We had already been assured of the former Miss Marianne Dashwood's surprising rally after her nearly fatal illness some three years ago. Instead of falling prey to gloom, dedicating herself to a solitary scholastic life, or even to contenting herself forever with exclusive devotion to her dear mother and younger sister, she had chosen rather to recognize her shortcomings and redirect her course. We had been alerted even then to her resolve to measure up to her sister Elinor's strictures for civil behavior in society. Nor could the wife of a Colonel John Brandon of Delaford, in Dorset, do other in such an elevated position.

Perhaps less acknowledged until now was that Marianne could not easily cast from her heart those indiscretions that had taken her to the brink of disaster with that unworthy gentleman, John Willoughby. And earnestly as she may now assure herself that she deplored her earlier folly, still, in sober effect, this passionate young person yet remained unable to fathom the exact nature of her own failings. Happily in this, her new, grander life, she was able as ever to give as impetuously—as much with her whole being—and now to a more grateful object. How fortunate for Mrs. Brandon that thus newly focused, her fervor could ensure her of flourishing in all her local undertakings.

Now barely twenty years of age, Mrs. John Brandon was a striking figure to look upon. To behold her on a fine, clear morning, gracious, glowing and zealous, walking out towards the village, moving with ease among the villagers, whether it be to ask after kin, or to dispense among the children her never-ending supply of two-penny cakes, was to believe that young Mrs. Brandon had been predestined for her present station. One could hardly wonder at the neighborhood's early embrace as a special favorite of such a mistress as she.

Consider now her power over Colonel Brandon himself. Here was a man much prevailed upon by life's iniquities. Observing him in the past, we had seen how eloquently his every movement reflected his heavy disappointment. Silent, solemn, dispirited, seldom ready for even a moment's play, he was then valued by his friends more for his solidity than his wit. Poor Brandon, was he not that very one, it had been scoffingly said, "whom everybody speaks well of, and nobody cares about"?

Yet, not very long after his beloved's decision to reward his fidelity, the good Colonel's transformation was complete. Melancholy was seen to be miraculously lifted from his countenance. Marianne's intensity effected so material a change that her husband was altered not only in stature—he stood taller and more commandingly—but an aspect that might even be deemed dashing overspread his face and figure. As his wife's devotion persisted, it even began to seem that the Colonel was restored to youth itself. Marianne, indeed, so warmed his character that his inclination to clothe himself in flannel waistcoats became one of the very earliest casualties of their union.

To any and all curious friends, Marianne would willingly recount the strange events leading to their own marriage. Her spirited talk—still displaying the usual want of caution—made her energetic in the telling of them.

"Yes, I will not deny it," she was wont to protest, her dark complexion shining, "in my first meeting with my dear husband, his reserve made him appear almost dull. But that was only at the beginning, and before I began to understand his quiet strengths, his elegant tastes, the genius guiding his sensible nature. I quickly took notice of my perceptive mother's urging of his virtues, how could I not? Besides this, how might I overlook my elder sister and new brother's eager sense of responsibility to this generous man? You must know that the Delaford living was his gift to them; furthermore, he had sought out the best artisans in the neighborhood, to secure the parsonage against draughts. I dare not so much as speak of his own good offices to myself in my great need. Soon I had no other course but to look upon him with favor. Now I can only wonder that he would have me at all! Has he not, after all, seen more than many a gentleman, traveled more widely than most? I assure you, few can equal him in knowledge or brilliance of spirit.''

Whether or not the ardent young lady exaggerated her husband's expansiveness, we must not contest. But one thing was evident, these remarkable new energies in the master of Delaford House *were* noticed, and welcomed by those upon his estate for whom he served as patron. For so many years before, while the Colonel's life was unsettled and sad, he had been abstracted or absent, or, when at Delaford at all, had shown little tolerance for the daily transactions of business.

His early disappointment in love had wounded him sorely, and his own solution for a broken heart was to avoid his native soil, to stay far away from the country dearest to him.

He had taken up his commission with the military, serving valiantly while his own regiment was stationed in the East Indies. Even after that engagement had been concluded, his disinclination to return home had determined his even longer absence in Bengal, in the wake of Hastings' departure. As to his leisure, his short leaves from the Regiment, they were more often spent in London, or in the company of one or another of his friends in the nearby countryside.

The Colonel was not altogether a careless landlord. Upon his coming of age, he had entrusted the management of his estate to his able steward, Mr. Stratton. Still, too soon after he reached his majority, and the villagers had celebrated their good fortune of acquiring such an upright young master, he had left English shores. It was years before the Colonel gave more than a merely proprietary glance to the conduct of his estate and farms at Delaford.

Now, with his marriage, and at the particular urgings of his loving wife—and what feats might he not attempt to please his dearest Marianne?—his view had altered. He alone must look to his property, oversee those lands more thoughtfully and regularly. He must finally take his proper position as a generous and tolerant patron.

There was little in the vicinity that might escape the notice of the master of Delaford, and soon his good sense and judgment was sought by cottagers and farmers alike.

Always a dedicated horseman, Colonel Brandon cut an imposing figure riding over his lands. Nor was his good impression merely one of appearance. He was energetic in seeking to assist his dependents, knocking on their cottage doors and offering charity to the least fortunate among them. Mr. Stratton had done what he could in his master's absence; still, what the Colonel saw in the rough habitations

of his villagers both touched his heart and brought
him to a new determination. He would now be in-
strumental in improving their lot as best he could.
In doing so, how might he not please his eager wife,
and serve them as well.

After his initial visits, and the effecting dispatch
with which he acted upon his plan, it was hardly
long before Colonel Brandon's reputation recovered, and soon enough his commitment to his estate
and its occupants went unquestioned.

This very morning, he sat at the table in his own
comfortable breakfast room before the fire, discoursing to his dear wife on this subject newly close
to his heart.

"Dearest Mrs. Brandon," said he, "a staircase is
such a rarity among the cottages, and how much it
could serve. These ladders they employ are a pos-
itive peril. Only yesterday, I watched as Mrs. Pet-
worth, carrying her infant in her arms, missed her
step, and nearly tumbled with babe together!"

Marianne was stirred by his anxiety. "How discerning you are," she cried. Of all the deprivations
the good village folk suffer, I expect this to be one
of the heaviest, especially for their women and the
littlest of them. There is nothing for it, my love.
They must have staircases; yes, they *shall* have
them; and as soon as they can be built, no matter
what the expense. I myself shall attend to it this
very morning."

The good Colonel, while admiring the warmth of
his wife's benevolence, nevertheless must needs
keep her enthusiasm in check.

"How your passion for their well-being does you credit," said he smiling. "But, once again, I must urge you to caution. You cannot have forgotten your last and admirably philanthropic venture to provide each cottage with its very own beehive. Sadly, the nature of small boys, armed with sticks, turned your honeyed scheme into chaos and stung limbs."

Marianne colored and would have retorted, but it was at that moment that their Mary announced the arrival of her sister, Elinor.

The sisters' greeting was of the warmest. Despite Elinor's many duties in the parish, there would hardly be a day, even in the foulest weather, when they did not visit together, or have the sight of one another at least. Their proximity was among the most fortunate benefits of their marriages.

"You are early this morning, sister," cried Marianne. "I pray that nothing is amiss?" For still her imagination would conjure drama at every turn.

Elinor's laughing assurances and tranquility provided comforting disappointment. Soon the good Colonel must leave them to confer with his steward on the construction plans for the cottages.

It was only then, considering the rather forward suggestion she wished to make, that Mrs. Ferrars felt herself able to explain to her sister her husband's travails amidst the church musicians.

"You will hardly think it, Marianne," concluded she, "but with the more serious difficulties facing Edward's flock he is altogether masterful in discovering ways to cope. It is these trifling matters that defeat him entirely."

"What trifling?" cried Marianne, her dark eyes ablaze with indignation. "This is insupportable! What can they mean by such impertinence, when our dear Edward is devoted only to their comfort, and does everything in his power to encourage their art? How ungrateful—nay, how unfeeling—to cause him such misery."

Marianne's instant decision in his favor, her breathless defense of her brother, did not surprise Elinor. Knowing Marianne as she did, she hastened to describe her method for their distraction, before her sister embarked upon something more extravagant. And her plan delighted Marianne.

"Dear sister, I shall suggest our stratagem to the Colonel immediately upon his return. We will arrange for your musicians an evening so gay, they will not soon know its like again. It will be the talk of the County, all elegance and vivacity. We shall invite our friends and all the neighborhood. Everyone must put on his very fashionable best for the occasion; you will see, the merrier the spectacle, the more we shall shame our music makers into good humor. You can be easy, and must leave the plan in my hands."

Elinor cherished the moment. Her sister may have been reluctant once to undertake such a post as mistress of Delaford; but established there, she would never allow reserve or spiritlessness in its management. Faults might be laid at Marianne's feet; yet reluctance to do battle on behalf of those she loved would never be one of them. So Elinor kissed her sister, and willingly put every reliance upon the success of their diversion.

4

Oftentimes an impossible person, even a chance event, can best meliorate a trying situation. At least, for Margaret Dashwood at Barton Park, this dictum proved stout. It was no less unlikely a benefactor than Mrs. Jennings, Lady Middleton's elderly mother, who effected the change.

This lady had taken prodigious care of the older Dashwood daughters in London long ago, and could, she felt, do no less for their younger sister. She took up residence at Barton for many months at a time, and was thus able to maintain her former ties to both remaining members of a family she now regarded as her very own. And though it may have continued precise to observe that Mrs. Jennings sometimes lacked taste, or even wit, she nevertheless could provide Margaret and Mrs. Dashwood the warmest reception for their frequent visits at the Park. Indeed, the reserve of the lady of Barton Park herself made her overtures increasingly welcome to them both.

More apposite yet was that above everything she genuinely valued, Mrs. Jennings venerated sociability about her; she was hungry for new acquaintance, for any stirring that might provide her excitement. If, in Lady Middleton's company, and in that of her irrepressible grandchildren—whom she too doted upon—even she comprehended that there was little civility to be sought, always she knew how dependably they could offer the comfort of bustle, and the deafening noise of spoilt children.

Most reliable for such lively engagements was their younger son, William Middleton. Since he was often quite overlooked by his mother in favor of her elder boy, he must make his presence felt. "Young John is, you see, such a perfect creature," Lady Middleton was given to pronouncing of her nine-year-old heir—and this well within the hearing of her younger boy—"yes, a resourceful, accomplished lad, and already so delightfully tall. Can you wonder that his brother must jump through hoops to equal him?"

Indeed, little William was often restive, noticeably fretful, and always troublesome. He devoted the better part of each day to making both brother *and* sisters miserable. In so short a span of life as his, this undertaking appeared to him the one entirely satisfying, so he pursued it with vigor. At just five years of age, the boy, it would appear, was especially gifted with agile legs and could exercise them handily to kick at their shins while yet remaining unobserved. Altogether swift, always precise, but never detectable, he then stood by, a contented ob-

server of all that ensued. Thus, each time the
screeching recommenced, and it did so regularly,
neither his mother nor grandmother could so much
as fathom what might have prompted it. But alas,
the wailing of Annamaria, John and Mary never left
off, and together with it, their bitter accusations
against this angelic little brother.

Poor Lady Middleton! There is no doubt that she
loved all her dears with an unstinting affection. Yet,
something perplexed, she must secretly wonder at
the true nature of the child's character.

"Might not the poor little fellow be lacking,"
she would hint—if only in the presence of her
good-natured mother—"in some property, dearest
Mama, that we all require in preparation for adult-
hood?"

The generally tranquil Mrs. Jennings tried, of
course, but could only be less than reassuring.

"Boys, my love," she began, "I, for one, know
very little of their rearing—a mysterious species altogether, I'll warrant you. From what I have seen
of the wild creatures, I can only wonder that *any*
are *ever* able to move towards gentility in manhood."

In all candor, for this good lady, what was the
most assuring presence by far within the Middleton
household, was that of her own dear son-in-law, Sir
John himself. He, she knew *must* provide diverting
associates for her pleasure. Like herself, he doted
upon the sight of young people—could not get
enough of them—at least when the season for hunting was not yet upon him. His zeal in the cause of

lively society she knew to be indefatigable, whether it be to put together an excursion for near strangers, to inspire a flirtation among them or to pursue, with a confidence directly proportionable to the young people's ignorance of his intention, arrangements for their nuptials. Such exertion served him as his happiest out-of-season diversion.

It was the very reason that Mrs. Jennings had made some arrangements of her own for this fortnight. With her son and daughter's leave, she had invited and was in expectation of receiving at Barton Park a pair of school friends, favorites she had not encountered for some time, each having gone her own way over the years. They were two ladies of some account, with whose affairs Mrs. Jennings had always concerned herself, whether they be near or far from her, and careless of whether or no they found themselves at leisure to spend their time with *her*. Her newest intelligence of them, which she had lately received with dismay, barely sweetened by hopes for future come-at-ability, was that like herself each of her former friends had been widowed.

Mrs. Jennings was much sorrowed by the sad turn in both of these lives dear to her own. One friend, she knew, who had lived most of her life in Somersetshire, had been left childless and alone; the other, having married a Frenchman, had been forced to return from France to her native land during the late turmoil and after the tragic loss of her noble husband. This second lady, however, *was* fortunate enough to be left with a fine son, a young man of some twenty-four or twenty-five years, who, she had heard, had already entered the army.

The feeling lady had, on the instant, determined now to do what it was in her power to do for both her former friends. Rather than proposing that they come to her solitary quarters in London, she offered what seemed a far livelier prospect. She felt certain that Sir John could introduce for them sparkling young company, organize for them delightful excursions in the country along with other extravagant distractions he was so expert at originating, to lighten their burden, to lift their spirits, and to divert them happily in Devonshire.

The first arrival of the pair was Lady Clara Ashburton. Though neither young nor precisely elegant, and with visage much subdued by misfortune, Lady Clara was tall, regularly handsome still, and had about her a quality that immediately engaged those she encountered. She knew how to listen, and did so diligently with everyone who might solicit her attention. When she spoke—and in that company it was hardly at all—it was with measured phrase. A comforting, but mostly silent lady, or so at least it looked to those who first attended her at Barton Park.

Her deference to the second boy of that boisterous family brought her immediate notice. When Lady Clara took an interest in William, how warmly did the child respond. He would chatter at her with every opportunity, challenge her, instruct her, demonstrate for her his prowess in running and riding. He persisted with grandiose boasts about his own muscular strength as exceeding even that of his older brother. And what solace her responsiveness gave to the boy! Novel it was to William to be so much as heard. He sought her out first the next day and would not willingly leave her side until his nurse commanded it. Most welcome of all to the company, this preoccupation of his with Lady Clara seemed to leave him less time to hatch mischief. It even began to appear that of a sudden, divine harmony might be anticipated within the nursery.

Clara Ashburton's patience with the child was admired; Mrs. Jennings pronounced her their heroine; and even Lady Middleton must acknowledge a notable slacking off in her children's rapturous exhibitions.

Mrs. Dashwood and her daughter had early been alerted to the coming of these two older ladies, and much had been made of their claims to gentility. In truth, they had been regaled for many days by Mrs. Jennings' recitation of these qualities.

"How I long for you to know them," she would begin, "these companions of my youth. I confess that though I have seen little of either since, never have I been in the least doubt of their devotion. Such grace and wisdom as theirs will, depend upon it, commend them to you entirely."

Though most willing to indulge Mrs. Jennings, as always, Margaret must still expect very little to interest her when she arrived that evening to meet one of these miracles. She was nevertheless ready to allow that her mother might be uplifted—first by

the opportunity to wear her best gown, and even
more by Sir John's having especially sent the carriage round to the cottage to fetch them. Such
attention was rare and ever gratifying to Mrs. Dashwood.

Imagine then Margaret's delight in finding in this
first new addition to their small circle a true benefit—a woman of education and sense. Silent she
may have remained in the presence of the earlier
company, but before very long Lady Clara had
made it perfectly clear that she was eager to converse with young Margaret. The recognition between them was immediate.

To be sure, discussion at table this evening had
commenced—as it must, for what could interest the
Middletons or their young caretaker, Margaret
more?—with appreciation of the latest marvels
from their young.

"Did you, my dear Lady Clara," began Sir John,
impatient to impress Mrs. Jennings' good friend,
"take note of my pretty little miss, Annamaria, ad-
monishing her serving girl? The child positively
will not be ruled. A proper young lady already, is
she not, my sweet girl? She will be governed by no
one but herself entirely, and she still so young."

To this, Lady Middleton must append news of
her own favorite.

"I tremble to think," said she, "what the boy
may yet achieve in life, when even now he shows
such valor in disciplining his new puppy. Did you
mark how he never tired at raising his stick?"

And since Mrs. Jennings too took pride in her
son and daughter's parental achievements, the sub-

ject proved inexhaustible. It took the party comfortably through most of their dinner.

It was only then that their visitor ventured comment. "We have indeed seen," said Lady Clara apropos, and with a meaningful glance, "how young William is coming alive. He positively delights in attention."

Margaret immediately understood her reference, and turning directly to her replied, "I myself, Madam, have been overjoyed to see the improvement in the boy's demeanor. His is a heavy lot. A third child can fall into veritable bafflement when his brother and sisters are such able, admired children. He will, the poor fellow, by nature consider himself unfit, incapable of doing anything with skill. It is something I, for one, am well acquainted with."

"Indeed," replied the lady with eager interest, "are you yourself then a third child?"

"The youngest," sighed she, "of three daughters."

Lady Clara could not but be amused. The sweet girl's half-serious, wry expression, and most of all weary tone made her smile. "Are your sisters then so superior in their undertakings that they overshadow your every act? I should hardly have guessed anything of the sort, my child," added the patient listener, "from the charming look of you. On the contrary, I expect *you* might come to notice in any society."

"Lady Clara, you are too kind. I begin to comprehend your unerring hand with young William Middleton. Still, were you acquainted with my elder sister Elinor, whose good sense and wisdom are awesome, or even my singular, whimsical sister Marianne, you should instead wonder at any sort of composure I might display.''

The older lady listened and admired. How philosophical about her family the young Miss Dashwood seemed. Hers was a delightful understanding, an awareness, a candor hardly expected in one so young.

Their exchange soon caught the attention of Mrs. Dashwood, who, upon hearing her elder daughters referred to, interrupted delightedly with proud intelligence about her own dears.

''Indeed, Lady Clara, here before you is only my very youngest. Two of my daughters are already established and married to gentlemen of some importance. How happy for us, is it not Margaret, that they are so settled, if at a distance from Barton, then at least within a mile of each other. But, dear Lady Clara, we are so fortunate as to visit them every now and again, and to find them both together, living comfortably upon the estate my second daughter's husband's at Delaford.''

''Are they actually one wed to patron and the other to parson at Delaford?'' asked Lady Clara astonished. ''And does one husband then serve another?—one sister serve another as well? If they remain yet on sisterly terms, they must be remarkable young ladies indeed.''

Mrs. Dashwood swelled with pride. ''My daughters are the most loving sisters, I assure you. In their respective stations, if one prove more elevated than the other, it can hardly come to notice between *my* dear girls.''

"Both young ladies, I assure you," Mrs. Jennings concurred, "are *now* much to be envied. If Mrs. Ferrars can not exactly be said to have chosen affluence, she seems comfortable enough for the present. But then, dear Lady Clara, there is Mrs. Dashwood's middle daughter, Marianne—surely one of the loveliest young women you will ever behold—and she, the very one we had near given up for lost, seeing her so lovesick and distraught, and finally in such deadly fever. My daughter Charlotte, even then expecting her second, and, I assure you, the most tender soul in all of creation, might one day relate for you the urgency of those dire circumstances at Cleveland. How we all trembled for Miss Marianne, thinking the most fearful thoughts! And now, here is she, mistress of a fine estate, and doted upon by our own stalwart friend, Brandon.''

It was not until the ladies had withdrawn, and upon Lady Middleton, Mrs. Jennings, and Mrs. Dashwood's having settled down together to continue, even then in the same vein, that Lady Clara and Margaret could turn to each other. They crossed the room to another sofa and there were able to talk quietly between themselves.

"I look heartily towards exploring your countryside, for I am an eager walker," Lady Clara began immediately. "Do you enjoy the outdoors, Miss Dashwood?''

"By my sister Marianne," replied Margaret smiling, "I was early taught nature's wonders; she and I would often walk in such a season as this, pursuing the dead leaves in their course on the wind. How she wondered at their liberty to whirl up and fly on the air! It was Marianne who first instructed me in how to view nature, to see its grandeur and its romance. Since that time, I have wandered everywhere in Barton Valley, often stopping to sketch what I see. While I dare not boast,'' with a saucy, conscious smile, ''of more than a shadow of my sister's lofty flights of fancy, I should nevertheless be honored, Madam, to show you about in the country I have come to know. I can assure you our neighborhood wants for nothing. What can be termed a simple road will be bounded by every variety of meadow and cornfield and rich woodland; there are saplings to be seen as well as venerable oaks and beeches nodding under their own weight.''

''What good fortune for me then,'' cried her Ladyship. ''These are delicious autumnal days indeed, when sometimes it feels milder even than in May. I do believe it was Mr. Burke who has taught us that 'art is man's nature.' I can think of nothing I should enjoy more than to accompany you upon one of your rambles, and if you are not unwilling, I shall take the liberty of watching you sketch, to study your own version of it.''

Margaret could hardly contain her pleasure at this exchange and promised faithfully to call for her new friend in the morning.

5

Early on the morrow, while Lady Clara and Margaret were still abroad, Mrs. Jennings' remaining guest arrived, nor was she alone. The Comtesse Isabel du Plessy startled and delighted Sir John by appearing in the company of her son, Lieutenant William du Plessy.

Stepping from her carriage in some state, assisted by this distinguished-looking young man, she received the immediate attentions of the Middletons' footmen and housemaids with an air of impatience. The Comtesse, in truth, was no longer young, and suffered from great fatigue; in the last days she had lacked her customary daytime rest. Still, her person was imposing, her dress fine; everything concerning the lady told of her importance.

Mr. du Plessy, once inside the house, did what he could to make his mother comfortable, hastily explaining that their journey had been eventful, thus full of delays, and each with its own vexatious consequence. As for the officer himself, it could not help but be noticed that he was a remarkably good-looking fellow. His stature alone might have caught all eyes, for he stood exceptionally tall; but then too, his manner of address and its thorough ease inspired immediate regard. These assets, when combined with that of a fair complexion and a spirited, even playful expression, must assure him of instant acceptance wherever he might choose to go. Barton Park, he appeared confident, would prove no exception.

Mrs. Jennings' welcome was of the most generous. It continued long after she had presented her new visitors to the household. She must certainly recalculate for them the number of years that had elapsed since their last meeting, a recollection difficult at best. Next, she could delight in the striking feat of the Comtesse's looks, remaining quite unaltered after so long an absence. Above everything, it was upon regarding the sturdy young person at her side that she must marvel at those extraordinary effects that only such passage of time may achieve in nourishing a babe into manhood. All this, as preface to her renewed compliments to her dear friend.

"Dearest Isabel," continued she, "as to yourself, you are of course perfection, as ever. We hoped to greet you the whole of yesterday. Our dear friend has this moment gone out walking in the countryside with one of our young ladies, and is thus not present to embrace you. Had we but known when you might finally make your appearance, she would surely have devoted the day to awaiting you. Still," she added, recovering her school-girl whisper, "we can together take our pleasure in observing her astonishment when she meets you first at dinner.''

Mrs. Jennings' effusiveness was not returned. During the length of this entire recitation, Comtesse du Plessy remained visibly out of countenance. She could hardly manage to hear the lady out, and finally she interrupted altogether, turning away to address her newly presented host.

"My good Sir John," she began with no delay, "how relieved I am to have reached your door safely after such a journey. You must already have been informed of our misfortunes. We were early beset en route by a carriage overturned directly in the middle of our road. Unhappy we were to see travelers injured and lying helpless in our path. Lord preserve us, they were so much in our way that there was simply no passing by them. Worse, my son must out the carriage to their assistance, and would persist, despite my own torments in such a situation. A monstrous inconvenience, I assure you, and every possible delay that a journey can occasion. Now, my good sir, I would impose even further upon your hospitality. My dear William, though he would soon return to his regiment, must indulge his mother yet awhile until I am quite recovered again from my travails. Though he had offered only to accompany me so far as Barton—and you see what good fortune it is that he has done so—I am, I find, yet unready to see entirely to myself. He shall, with your permission, rest a little still, before he quite abandons me in favor of the army.''

Sir John bowed at the graciousness of this

speech. He was secretly pleased to have acquired both such a noble guest *and* her esteemed son, and gave every assurance that nothing could give him greater pleasure. The lady was next gathered up by the ever-patient Mrs. Jennings, accompanied by nearly every servant at the Park, to be seen to her quarters and her much-needed repose.

For the two gentlemen, this removal presented the opportunity to withdraw themselves to the study for a brandy. The master of Barton Park was, in truth, anxious to learn all the particulars concerning such an unexceptionable young man, whose appearance so entirely favored him. He had barely sat him down, glass in hand, before his inquiries commenced regarding the nature of his commission, the state of his regiment, and where they were currently located. And the agreeable Mr. du Plessy was quite ready to oblige.

"I serve, good Sir," began he, "with my regiment, the Fourteenth Dragoons, which is now encamped just outside the city of Brighton. And indeed it is there that I must return before the fortnight is out."

"Brighton, is it," said Sir John, "how I myself do prefer it to Cheltenham or Scarborough. But in all candor, good sir, I will admit that I don't much fancy all those *spaws,* let fashion be hanged. I cannot abide the waters. What with all these goings on, one would sometimes think that Englishmen were ducks, ever waddling to their waters. No, no, my good sir, none of it suits me one whit."

Bethinking himself, he then leaned towards the

young man with a half smile, and clearly intent upon enjoying the moment whispered, "But I wager you turn many a pretty head in that quarter. Now I think on it, what better fortune for one so young than to be stationed in Brighton! I warrant you that every fashionable young heiress mustn't fail to be seen in the assemblies there at least once in a season, if not more. And," looking devilish, he offered, "this surely is not to speak of the much that is made of the many diversions more recently to be found there—all for the sake of the Prince Regent's own devotion to *the waters*. You can not, I am sure, want for amusement on *any* night of the week!"

Barely had du Plessy opportunity to dissent—he had seen little enough of that great spa's pleasures—when Sir John protested anew, in the same confiding tone.

"My dear Sir, here at Barton we can, I fear, offer you no such dazzling entertainment. But if you are a sporting man—and how might I doubt of that form the look of you—we can serve you admirably. To my mind," he persisted, "there is no more manly amusement than the hunt, would not you agree? I repeat it often enough to Lady Middleton, and she agrees with me every time I take the subject up! Moreover, I would say it firmly to any man: to ride to hounds, to expect every minute a bold reynard to break away, to course over this, the finest country in the kingdom, that, my friend, is sport! I can assure you, moreover, that there is no corrective better for those otherwise depraved influences overspreading all of dear England nowadays. Yes, indeed, the tally-ho! *only* the tally-ho is the call *we* respond to. That harmonious ring in the open air, I tell you, it is magic—a national preservative. Yes, a national preservative! Where, my dear sir, might we in England be today without the sport?"

Finally, perceiving a lull, Mr. du Plessy was able to give every assurance that his inclinations—both for riding to hounds and, more particularly, towards the valiant preservation of the stamina of the kingdom—were of the best, if indeed he had himself had little opportunity in his short history to pursue that passion.

"My own family, Sir John," began the young man, "was allowed few such pleasures. But then, our particular fortunes were so much occupied by the events about us, the constant ruptures, the changes imminent, how could we? We scarcely knew where we might be next. And though my own dear French father was ever devoted to the sport, he had little leisure to instruct his eager son. Yet I am a keen horseman, and always ready for the exhilaration of hunting. For the honor you bestow I am grateful too, and have every intention of taking up your kind invitation while I am here at Barton Park."

Sir John was obviously pleased to find this elegant young officer so receptive. Encouraged, he would embark once again, and even more at length upon another of his grievances—how lacking was the nation in civility in these reduced times—when, glancing out the salon window, the generous host was startled to espy none other than his young friend Margaret Dashwood just then escorting Lady Clara back to the house after their morning's ramble.

This missing pair had wandered happily together in the vast parkland surrounding Barton, chatting comfortably, stopping upon each rise where nature provided the full splendor of the season. The older lady was content to observe as the younger sketched the fine light and shade of the landscape before her. So had they walked for several hours, until Clara Ashburton pronounced herself quite ready to turn back in sweet exhaustion.

Margaret was thus taken quite unawares to hear Sir John summoning her to join him immediately in the study. After her excursion, she could think only of returning to Barton Cottage, where she was awaited by her mother. Still, since their arrival some years ago, she had come to understand their benevolent patron. She knew him energetic when inspired. Resistance, she had already seen, would only spur him the more. Entering the room, and startled by the presence of the stranger, she could but smile to herself as she comprehended Sir John's urgency. His head afire with potential, he must be the first to rush forward. Here before her now was one of his promising inventions.

Generally of a cheerful disposition, Margaret found herself particularly so today after her walk. The brisk wind had brought color to her cheeks. And if her hair was windblown and her gown muddied as she entered the room, there was all the same a radiance about her.

Lady Clara had struck her as someone taken from a favorite book, a creation perhaps of one of the older poets, so great was her sense of serenity. The lady was grateful for every new discovery—none was too small to go unappreciated—whether it be Margaret's calling attention to the sprays of broom just barely visible along the path, or a stand of hazel at the water's edge. Moreover, whatever she acquainted her with, she listened with an attentiveness that convinced her guide of her knowledgeability, even of her superior powers in observing nature. That was Lady Clara's particular gift to those who knew her. She was one of those blessed few who continued in age with a youthful characteristic in her disposition, that of surprise. She even confessed to waking each day in expectation of learning something new. It had delighted Margaret that morning to provide the means.

As for Sir John, he could hardly have been more effusive. Said he, in a significant tone, as if delivering to her a gift, "My dear child, may I present to you our noble friend, Mr. William du Plessy?"

The young officer, himself startled, immediately rose to greet her. She could see that he too was bewildered, and for some moments hardly a word issued from his lips, yet the while his eyes rested firmly, intently, upon her. It seemed a long time before his look gave way and he regained his composure sufficiently to remark that he had little notion that by delivering his mother to her aging

school friends he should find the circle to include
one of such youth and beauty.

"You will forgive me if I seem overwhelmed,"
he said, with an amused eye, "I hardly expected to
find myself dazzled by one of Mrs. Jennings' companions." His gaze persisted even as he listened to
Sir John explain Margaret's sudden appearance before them.

"Why, my good sir, surely you know that the
Dashwood family, formerly of Norland Park in Sussex, is our kin. They have for some time graced our
surroundings, though we now number fewer of
them among us. I always say that any might fall in
love with Margaret's mother, Mrs. Dashwood, and
Margaret's fine sisters have each abandoned our table and hospitality to marry well. They are become
Mrs. Brandon and Mrs. Ferrars of Delaford in Dorset. Still," he added significantly, "you see here
before you our beautiful youngest Dashwood."

So he continued while Margaret's discomfort increased. She felt her color rising the more, and
wished only to be away, to return to her mother in
peace. But Sir John, she knew, would not allow it,
especially with such a sturdy find as this. He was,
as always, inspired to join the whole universe into
the happy state of matrimony.

Mercifully, the gentleman, seeing her embarrassment, intervened to divert his purpose. Said he,
"Miss Dashwood, are you then a great walker in
the country?"

"I take my exercise whenever the weather al-
lows. It keeps me hale," was all she could manage.

He then talked of the outdoors, of the pleasures of greeting the seasons the country provides. His eloquence and open manners, she thought, could commend him to any woman. In truth, his person brought back to her another, someone she remembered, especially when he would, after such a brief moment's acquaintance—and without the least hesitation—engage her in walking with *him*.

"I expect, since you are devoted to your daily excursions, you can better than anyone else introduce me to your splendid country and all its hidden wonders. Might I ask for your assistance in this?"

Sir John, upon hearing his suggestion, was aglow.

She was, however, perplexed by the directness, the hastiness of such a suggestion, its lack of reserve. Mr. du Plessy, it was clear, was used to saying and doing just as he wished. Yet whatever she might feel as to its propriety, in the presence of their kind benefactor her own manners might prove less than perfect if, upon being thus appealed to, she answered in the negative.

And so it began.

6

Dinner was *the* most interesting action of any day for Lady Middleton. After the travails she so regularly underwent, it restored to her the serenity, the gaiety, for which she knew herself renowned, even—if with something less frequency—the wit. This evening, with such an array of illustrious visitors joining her at Barton Park, she could anticipate all these blessings together; and thus began her morning to a great business and stir.

Memorable evenings at the Park, the lady supposed to depend solely upon her own efforts. It was she who thought hard before fixing upon the china suitable to the occasion; who scrutinized for spotted glassware; and who lectured the butler sternly on promptness in the delivery of his announcements. She alone was mindful of how inept servants could reduce feast to fiasco.

Her most strenuous efforts of all, she knew, must center this evening upon the provision of exquisite culinary choices and their combination into an har-

monious repast. And while her attention had all of
yesterday been firm upon Lady Clara, her emphasis
now shifted to the new arrival. The Comtesse du
Plessy would have known—certainly until the time
of her family's misfortune—the finest French cuisine. Lady Middleton ever fancied herself possess-
ing the very best table that any family might offer
in Devonshire, and today could not, would not, tol-
erate any potential insufficiency to emerge in the
presence of such formidable company.

"Unity, integrity, my dear Mrs. Ely," the knowledgeable lady reminded her head cook, "they are
everything to those who are schooled in ceremony.
Your venison may be done to a turn, your gravies
irresistible, but, my good woman, they will be nothing without those exact, those masterful French vin-
tages cunningly selected for the purpose. Nor shall
our service at Barton ever, I quite assure you, do
without several removals from table—those many
inimitable courses—certainly not when *our* guests
have been seen in your grander houses, and most
particularly in the best ones on the Continent."

Thus it was that by evening the Lady had
achieved every possible miracle, and stood content
with her labors. She had also commanded the full
devotion of her maids, been attended to as to her
person, her hair, and in the matter of choosing a
dress. She appeared serene in her latest acquisition,
one of the more romantic style now becoming fashionable, a white muslin adorned with a lace ruff
high about her neck, and just visible as she moved
was an enchanting Grecian bend to her skirt.

She could, in high state, greet each of her guests as they appeared. And it was her good fortune that the Comtesse du Plessy and her so exceptionally well-favored son—the more dashing this evening in a precisely cut coat of the military style, along with a cravat tied to perfection—descended first, and that they could command her every courtesy.

"I trust, Madam," she began, "now you are recovered from your wearisome journey, you can happily devote yourself to the delectations of dining at Barton."

Herself attired in her own finest gown, the Comtesse looked doubtful, but nevertheless signaled her assent. Yet, upon seeing Mrs. Jennings just then entering the room arm-in-arm with their friend Lady Clara, she stepped abruptly away, quite deserting her startled hostess in favor of her old acquaintances.

The reunion of the ladies was so merry and sweet-humored as almost to defy good breeding. All three took hands and expressed the greatest of satisfaction at seeing each other again. Even the Comtesse, always superior—a model of composure—was for this moment undermined by the sight of her childhood playmates. She too was heard to join in their familiarity.

"Did I not assure you, dearest Clara," was Mrs. Jennings' triumphant interjection, "that you must be thoroughly astonished at Isabel's elegance? How far we have come from the gawkish girls at the academy, to be sure."

"Hardly astonished," was Lady Clara's smiling

response, "Isabel was ever the most fashionable of
us all. But I am more pleased," added she in a
lower voice, "to see my friend in such excellent
figure. And especially, dear Comtesse, after all that
you have endured."

"You must tell us your secret, dearest, decorous
Isabel," Mrs. Jennings demanded, and in so affectionate a tone that even the Comtesse was surprised
into enthusiasm and shook her head, protesting
gently, while displaying to its best effect her coif-
fure.

It began to seem that these old friends had little
use for another in their converse. Throughout Mrs.
Jennings' energetic compliments and the Comtesse's even more vigorous denials, Lady Middleton
and her husband were left to stand in silence, neglected despite the perfection of her Ladyship's
appointments. Only Mr. du Plessy found some diversion in these proceedings, especially while es-
pying the animation of his mother in this unseemly
display.

It was Lady Clara who finally observed the discomfiture of her host and hostess, and was embar-
rassed. As remedy, she promptly proposed to her
noble friend that they all enjoy a tour about the
beautiful Middleton house.

The Comtesse, recalled by this suggestion to her
more usual arrogance, readily agreed. Truth to tell,
she was as yet not prepared to seat herself upon the
sofa, or to devote her exclusive attention to her
hostess. She strolled about instead, her quizzing
glass raised to her eyes, edifying the company by

her astuteness in such matters as judging the craftsmanship and authenticity of each piece of the Middletons' furniture and every painting upon their walls. Happily, Sir John was oblivious to any slight. He was content to display these splendors, discoursing readily upon the history of his family and its many generations of shrewd acquisition.

All this disquiet, this prancing to-and-fro, could well have continued much longer had the butler not interrupted with word that the ladies from Barton Cottage had just made their entrance. Indeed, the Middletons' carriage had once again been dispatched for Margaret and her mother in a hasty recall, after last night's dinner had not succeeded in including amongst them their grandest visitors, the du Plessys. So these friends proved of immediate service tonight by rescuing the entire company from their extended ambles to join them in the sitting room.

Immediately upon the two ladies' presentation, the Comtesse studied them and—not unlike her earlier perusal of Barton Park itself—turned her glass slowly downwards to take in the whole. Her condescension remained affable, but it was too soon evident that her curiosity regarding them was simply not aroused; she had little to say to either and brusquely turned her attention elsewhere. Her son, however, was more forthcoming, even eager to greet these charming new additions to their party. Sir John had barely completed his introductions before the young man addressed the older of the ladies.

"Mrs. Dashwood," cried he, "this very afternoon I had the honor of intercepting your lovely daughter upon her return from the woods. It was as though a nymph from a pastoral world had appeared to greet me. So she seemed. But now that I meet her parent," with a bow, "I comprehend her look the better."

Margaret turned away, mortified at the too much warmth of the young man's speech. But Mrs. Dashwood—who had learned from her daughter only that the Comtesse had appeared accompanied by a son—was altogether engaged. She had been quite unprepared for the striking look of the gentleman, and that look—coupled with so jaunty an address—captivated her.

"Perhaps you yourself, Sir," she responded lightly, "have been taken in by some mischievous spirit from our nearby forest—I am assured that there are some hereabouts—for I cannot, upon my life, imagine how we simple folk in the country might be regarded by such a man of the world as yourself—especially as I am told you were reared upon the Continent."

Their pleasantries could not but catch the ear of the lieutenant's mother, who looked towards her son more than once to wonder what could possibly be a source of gaiety on that side of the room. Until then, she herself had been holding forth to the company upon a subject most dear to her heart, the many melancholy alterations her sudden removal from France had imposed. But the Comtesse du Plessy, who had ever preferred her son's charming attentions and courtly manners to that of any other being in the world—would miss not a moment of them—thus gladly interrupted herself in midsentence, to turn instead towards him and the ladies sitting by him to bring forward her own discourse. Nor would its lack of relevance to their converse deter her, for she had quite determined they must join in *her* exchange.

"And can you, Mrs. Dashwood," demanded she, "so much as imagine the loss that was ours upon leaving that exalted society? Can you fathom the deprivation? Ah, my dear William, you will recall the sophistication of speech and gesture so notable among our former countrymen. The soirees in gardens, the salons of the Trianon, not to speak of the theatricals—ah, such evenings as were! You must understand, Mrs. Dashwood, customs of liveliness, mirth, of especial civility could thrive upon the Continent. I confess, in returning here—as dear as England is to myself—I have had, alas, to make my adjustments. No, I fear there can be no more of the grandeur that once we knew."

All of the company, at first dazzled, was sobered by this fearful prediction. It particularly stilled Mrs. Dashwood and the officer's frivolity, and they too were brought to gloomy silence.

Only Lady Clara, heretofore merely looking on, must now laugh aloud at such large comparisons. "Dear Comtesse," she queried her old friend, "could all of England then be wholly lacking in manners, without cultivation or taste? There must surely be some to be sought in the land," she added, "if not in all the country, or even in London, then at least," with a gesture towards her hosts, "in preferred parts of it."

"Not in any part," replied the Comtesse. "Depend upon it, Lady Clara, you will seldom discern in the English drawing room the kind of manners we were come to expect daily at Court."

Her son was pained by his mother's rudeness; but Sir John, ever genial, quickly stepped forward to agree with his guest.

"Aye, you shall find us a hearty, if rustic crowd; yet we can but hope that your presence, Madam, may uplift us. My English countrymen are, I assure you, not unlike myself, ever willing to learn."

Yet the Comtesse was not to be appeased or deterred. She assured Sir John that her disappointments upon her return to her native land were sore indeed. *She* had been brought back to a world of the ill-bred, a people nearer to vulgarity than to civilized behavior.

"And this, from such a place as Paris," concluded she. "But all is now destroyed, I fear. And you must know that every single bit of it stems from what is reverently termed a revolutionary spirit— that license, that disgraceful new liberality that we most recently have come to assume to be so very good when displayed by our young. It is this that has ruined gracious society in France. I, for one, will not answer for what is to become of any of us, if indeed events continue as they have."

Young du Plessy was oddly relieved at the turn in his mother's recitation. Having attended many times her disquisitions upon the decline of civilization, he had learned that lamentation upon the general, rather than a tally of its particulars, was at least the less offensive. And once the conversation had resumed, he promptly managed to separate himself from it just sufficiently to address a comment in Margaret's direction. It was merely a half-whisper, but she heard him clearly enough.

"Miss Dashwood," he offered, "I prefer to see it as my own good fortune to be detained quite suddenly here at Barton to look to my mother's indisposition. Else, and I shudder to think of it, we should not have met at all and become acquainted."

Once again, he had succeeded in startling her by the extravagance of his address. What could he mean by it? His earlier flattery of her mother, she had barely countenanced. This sally she could check only with a low-voiced protest that, so far as she knew, they had barely met, and most certainly not as yet become acquainted.

He seemed taken by surprise; but smiled in some amusement and quickly admitted to the distinction. "Not *yet* become acquainted. At least, Miss Dashwood, I welcome your contemplating such a possibility for the future. Of course," becoming on the instant grave, "you are correct in your reproof. Courtesy might indeed have demanded that I mention merely the prospect of becoming acquainted with your exquisite countryside, rather than the fair instructor by whose means I hope to explore it. For it is true that I have long heard of Devon's own wildness, its remarkability, its variety, its perfection. I trust it not altogether improper of me to desire that it be under your direction that I become familiar with its wonders.''

''Surely, Sir, an ambitious design for one here so little time. Your regiment must soon require your services; I can hardly imagine your achieving familiarity anywhere in Devonshire, however nimble your ability.''

Her words were designed to rebuff; but the young man answered eagerly. ''How true, Miss Dashwood, and but for that harsh fact, I would not be so bold as to ask for your special attention so soon after our meeting. Since my visit must be but brief, I must needs be forward.''

This last rendered Margaret speechless. Rarely had she heard such liberty of address from a gentleman before, and never, certainly, from the young gentlemen she encountered hereabout. Such talk, if proper enough perhaps in a Frenchman, still possessed for her an ill-fitting air of mischief. Mr. du Plessy meant undoubtedly to disarm every objection—*and* was entirely confident that he could do so with any lady.

Margaret however, saw through his rakish manner. ''I expect your native pace exceeds our own,'' said she. ''Here in the country, we rush into very little, making our plans only as fast as we must, however appealing such a request may be. In the fashionable world, Sir, perhaps you are more accustomed to act upon whim, lest you miss any of the new pleasures that come your way. We can only trust you now show patience with us slower country people.''

He started at this, chastened. ''How little you comprehend of my appeal, Miss Dashwood. I am a mere soldier and I must ask for your generosity. We who have lived in turbulence are now pledged to reclaiming what we can of life. My own youth, so full of loss, so changeable, has, I sometimes fear, made me too eager, too impetuous. Forgive my display of haste in matters unrelated, matters that should never be so approached. But it is of no importance...''

How serious he had suddenly become. There might, for all his fair words, be qualities in him after all.

And when she agreed to keep her earlier promise to escort him the very next day for an excursion to Barton's more hidden parkland—being scrupulous to add only that he might make a third of a party to join Lady Clara and herself—she watched with some amusement as he drew himself in and allowed not so much as a flicker of disappointment to be visible in his aspect.

7

"**I** do believe," began Mrs. Dashwood, addressing her daughter at breakfast the very next morning, "that Sir John and Lady Middleton quite exceeded themselves last night in their liberality. The widgeon and the preserved ginger were as exquisite as one could wish; the red currant sauce over the tongue as delectable. Nor had I—and I am willing to confess it—anticipated such august company. It was, was it not, an occasion to remember?"

Upon this matter, for once Margaret must agree with her mother. Diversion during the evening had not been lacking, and Lady Middleton's efforts as hostess, if nothing else, had succeeded in producing delicate fare. Most gratifying had been the opportunity to strengthen her friendship with Lady Clara, discovering a warmth the sweeter for seeing the other lady felt it too. She could now express her own feelings without hesitation. The evening had been unexceptionable.

Thus encouraged did Mrs. Dashwood persist,

happily rehearsing the whole of the event—her every movement from the point of her being assisted into the Middleton landaulette to admire its veneering—through to the finery of the pearl bandeaux ornament gracing Comtesse du Plessy's hair. Naturally, from then she must progress to a study of the costume of all the ladies in attendance. It was her joy so to do. For Mrs. Dashwood, the grandness of such entertainments was a subject to exult over. It gave her reassurance that when she herself had chosen to come away so distant with her young daughters to her cousins in Devonshire, there had been no loss of elegance in the removal, even by comparison with evenings at their own stately Norland whilst her husband had lived.

Margaret rejoiced to see her mother in such cheerful spirits, and was ready to agree with her every observation. It was only when Mrs. Dashwood's rehearsal turned to a more particular appreciation of the other guests that she felt unease.

"The Comtesse," cried the lady, "is imposing, to be sure; and her young lieutenant as well-bred a gentleman as I have encountered. Was he not, dear Margaret, a surprising and most welcome addition to our party? In truth, my child, we *are* fortunately situated here at Barton, after all. I have not, I assure you, seen a livelier or a more delightful evening at the Park, or met so engaging a young man since your dear father was eligible."

At these words, Margaret lowered her eyes and tried to conceal a blush. For fairness' sake alone, it must be avowed that Mrs. Dashwood was not one of those many parents who dedicate themselves solely to seeking out prospective husbands for their daughters.

This sweet-natured lady, after all, could remember—and that, not so long ago—her early fears for the future of all her dear girls after the death of their father. Her hopes had been simply to provide excellent circumstance for them to flourish in—superb society both for herself and her children. It was concern for their happiness alone that had propelled her every action. Yet she, like any other, when faced by suavity and flair, was hardly less susceptible to suggestion. Besides, the young officer had caught her fancy.

It was when Margaret had confessed to her mother her own promise to Mr. du Plessy of an afternoon's outing in the company of Lady Clara that it began to seem to our heroine that there was no cease to her mother's interest.

"What good fortune, Margaret," she cried, "to make such an acquaintance. The young man is, I believe, eager to please. He wishes to give delight to ladies, and better still, he is altogether adept in its delivery. You must endeavor to learn of his pursuits, his diversions, and above all else, the dishes he most fancies. If his disposition is as easy and attractive as it appeared last night, we will ourselves return the compliment by asking him to dine with us here at the cottage before his departure for Brighton. I am quite willing to display for him my skills at table, my very own specialities in what I believe he himself might call *cuisine*. We must, you know, do what we can for our officers.''

Margaret, though contented as ever with her gentle mother's sociability, must all the same feel trepidation as she listened to this impetuous proposal. She had witnessed such expansiveness in her indulgent, impractical mother before. She could recall years ago how recklessly Mrs. Dashwood had embraced—how unhaltingly encouraged—her poor sister Marianne into first love—even grand passion for Mr. Willoughby. Not once had she recognized *any* insincerity in the demeanor of that false young man. Even today, Margaret fretted over this lack in her mother. It seemed that Mrs. Dashwood could even yet rush headlong towards novelty wherever she fancied she had met it; she remained capable of admiring impudence as directness, audacity as wit, impropriety as imagination. And not unlike her own dear Marianne, she was still as susceptible to fantasy as ever she had been before.

Yet what a contrast was there to be seen in her now-grown youngest! Those years ago, while still under the strict tutelage of her sister Marianne, the impressionable Margaret had herself been altogether smitten by that same ''preserver'' of her revered sister. Though none of her intimates had so much as taken note of it, she too had fallen in love with John Willoughby—and that as only a thirteen-year-old could do.

He had become as dear to her, in truth, as any first love, for he was her sister's savior, her knight in armor. Only later, observing Marianne's anguish, had Margaret suffered the sting—altogether in silence, and without help from her family.

The affair had cost this most innocent of the sisters the loss of her every illusion. A mere child, she had been at first stunned, then truly afflicted by the discovery of the immense power she saw in such a loving attachment. Herself heartbroken, she began to comprehend how such treachery in a seemingly upright young man might altogether destroy the hardiest of beings.

Margaret would, during that time, have gladly turned for help to her eldest sister. She knew Elinor to be endlessly brave—heroic, even—and above all, superior in good sense. But in truth, what she feared was finding her too-serious, even stern sister less so in patience or wit. It was Elinor's reserve that the child found intimidating; she trembled that yet again she would be laughed at, dismissed for her own simplicity, her foolishness. For Margaret, there was little comfort to be found anywhere.

Thus, from an early age, our heroine, tossed rudely from dependence upon her good sisters into the greater world, determined upon making her own decisions, vowing that *she* would ever seek her own path forward. At least, she had come to understand this: that she need not again allow herself to be taken in by boldness, by chivalric bravado—no matter how attractive the author of it might appear. The never-ending supply of suitors put forward by Sir John had since provided ample opportunity to stand fast in her decision.

As for du Plessy, it was in his facility in the

drawing room above all that Margaret Dashwood had detected just such a danger. His certainty of success with every lady there must condemn him in her eyes. Such a lack of formality was in all his converse, a carefree manner, a freedom and familiarity that would suggest he had known them intimately all their lives. Indeed, it was the very charm, the seeming frankness of his style that had given her pause. He seemed genuine enough; but was he not merely toying with the provincials as he idled for a few days at Barton?

Du Plessy's ease had clearly charmed her mother; it might well bring both Sir John and Lady Middleton to their feet; it could even succeed in keeping his own arrogant, pretentious mother at his beck and call; but as to her own person, he would find in her a harder case. Courteous she would be—as a guest of their patrons the Middletons she owed him that—but all the while wariness itself.

And as she dressed for their excursion to Pocombe Bridge, she chose to think no more of the intrusive young officer, but only of the pleasure which awaited, and of Lady Clara's express desire to find the county's most treasured landscape.

The bridge at Pocombe, Margaret knew well and was certain that its enchanting arches over the stream, its pellucid water with its level ever-rising, and its banks so clear and smooth, together with a view of the deserted abbey nearby, must delight her friend as they did herself. She had designed that they were to spend the afternoon on a lane not much frequented, under the shade of the elms, and by the side of that brimming Exe where all is pleasing to the eye.

As to William du Plessy, he was as good as his word, and awaited her in the drawing room. They were soon joined by Lady Clara, whose surprise at this addition was visible for the merest instant only. He, however, bowed graciously and addressed the lady directly with, "I hope, Madam, that this intrusion on my part will not diminish your own pleasure in the outing. I shall merely accompany you and observe, with not a word spoken on my part. Miss Dashwood will teach us, I trust, where to look."

So all three embarked together on this fortunate day, when the air, the sky and earth seemed lulled into an universal calm, accompanied by soft sunshine and falling leaves of every color around them. Lady Clara, ever practical in her pursuit of natural beauty, would begin by reminding the gentleman that theirs must be a leisurely pace.

"You will understand, Sir, and be patient. I do not manage your stride, nor possess the vigor of youth. Still, we shall progress admirably, if you will offer me your arm. Miss Dashwood contrives for my sake to stop often while I gather breath. This she refers to as time for taking a sketch of that vista or this bend in the lane, until I am again ready to proceed. You, I expect, shall entertain us with uplifting comment at such points. I assure you, we are quite prepared to listen."

The officer obeyed and the two walked arm-in-arm with Margaret beside them, all the while call-

ing their attention to the various birds, to the low
furze bursting even now with golden blossoms, and
to the abbey above the hill, with its sky fair and the
clouds swift in their movement beyond it.

They continued contentedly until the older lady
was ready to rest, and the three settled comfortably
near to one another while she regained her breath.
Their silence was easy, for there was much to observe; none felt the want of unnecessary speech.

Only after some minutes did Lady Clara, recalling with amusement her exchange with his mother
the evening before, address the young man with
curiosity.

"Are you then, Sir, also of a mind with your
good mother regarding a lack of civility in us poor
English? Do you too find us without refinement?"

Mr. du Plessy was openly abashed by this recollection of the Comtesse's condescension. "My
mother, dear Madam, cannot but regret our tragic
history. Still, she grieves for a society that may now
seem grander than it once was. It is true that Paris
life was unlike any other. She remembers the once
peaceful strolls upon the tree-lined avenues, the elegant salons. She thinks of her high bonnets and
their impeccability as the mark of fashion. What she
prefers not to recall is the roar of the tumbrels. Yet
she is not to be reprimanded, and certainly by myself, if her own unhappiness over the untimely loss
of my father has overtaken her judgments. She
would, I fear, wish the solution were simply to be
found in a setting back the clock."

He spoke haltingly but with intensity. There was

little jauntiness now in him, and none of the draw-
ing-room polish Margaret had seen last night. In
truth, he showed to his mother's old friend an altered mood. "As to my own alliances," continued
he, "*I* will remember each indignity, every humil-
iation to which my dear father was put, even before
his end. And yet though my name, dear lady, be
French, with all my heart I am English. This fair
island I hold as dear as does any of my countrymen,
and no prouder boast have I than that I have fought
in Spain under the great general himself, Wellesley,
he who might properly be called the flower of our
own English aristocracy. Miss Dashwood, I do indeed soon return to my regiment, and it is with
some pride that I do so."

Lady Clara listened in admiration to the young
officer's speech, and Margaret herself, noting the
transformation in his demeanor, found the alteration
distinctly perplexing.

It was only upon their return hours later to the
great house, after bidding farewell to the fatigued
Lady Clara, that the subdued young officer finally
addressed himself directly to his guide.

"I trust you will allow me to tell you, Miss Dashwood, how this glorious afternoon in the countryside will sustain me as I rejoin my regiment. I shall
keep you"—and checking himself, he added, "and
good Lady Clara, of course—most warmly in my
thoughts as we once more engage in our struggle."

Her color rose; but softened, Margaret managed
to respond as graciously as she could before making

her retreat towards the cottage. There was more to
Mr. du Plessy than she had anticipated.

At the door, she found Mrs. Dashwood cheerily
greeting her while holding out a letter that had just
arrived from Dorset. Marianne had addressed her
mother and sister, as follows:

*Behold me, dearest Mama and Margaret,
for I am now going to write you as handsome
a letter as I can! I have so many little matters
to tell you of that I hardly know where such
delights must begin.*

*Have I, dear ones, as yet revealed to you
that my valiant Colonel has engaged a renowned painter to make a portrait of his lady
wife?*

*You can be sure that in my new spotted mus-
lin I shall be very proper, grand, and even
stately in the sittings. Then this solemn new
opus shall hang in our long corridor among
all those others, those surly dark figures, the
early Brandons.*

*And now, perhaps, to the best of all news.
We are to be giving a ball at Delaford within
the fortnight! Need I alert you to the circumstances which necessitated our decision to
plan it so inconveniently in this awkward mid-
season? It is, I assure you, quite important to
do so, and without delay. You must know that
dear Edward's musicians of late have been
quite unable to perform for him in church on
Sundays. These artisans, it would seem, cannot*

*so much as be in one another's presence with-
out quarrels and bitterness amongst them. Our
magnificent project will mend all that, you
shall see, and they will straightaway be all
harmony. But you will know all as soon as you
are come.*

*Do come to us, won't you, for we shall very
much require your presence for the festivities.
And please do so as soon as you may.*

Yours very affectionately,
Marianne

Margaret perused her sister's letter with delight.
Enticing was the promise of the ball, and more attractive to her still was the immediate prospect of
escape from Devonshire. Well she knew that Mr.
du Plessy's persistent attentions towards her could
surely not go unremarked for much longer by the
good-willed but incorrigible Mrs. Jennings and her
staunch ally, Sir John—if indeed they had until
now. And how might she expect to be left in peace
at Barton Park for the next several days, or even—
for their memory was long—well after all these
guests had departed?

More troubling perhaps, was that Margaret herself, after observing the officer in his earnest converse with Lady Clara today, had, despite every
resolve, begun to view him in a more favorable
light. The very idea made her anxious. She would
be away.

"Dearest Mama," cried she, "Please do let us
go, and soon."

"But, of course, my sweet, you will wish to attend your sisters' festivities; why such haste? Can not we wait yet a week at least before we depart for Dorset, now we are favored with such superior society at Barton Park? Take leave of your own Devon! Was not your wandering and your company entirely satisfactory this afternoon?"

Margaret must of course promptly assure her mother that, quite to the contrary, her excursion had been pleasing in every particular. She recounted their rambles by the river, the natural beauties that had unfolded before them, and Lady Clara's delight in all. Of the officer, she preferred, however, to say nothing.

Happily, Mrs. Dashwood's attentions were already upon her own plans. She did not notice the omission. "I confess," she said, "I had quite hoped, even expected, that we could be with our dear girls, your sisters, before Martinmas; but alas, how might I go so soon as this? You must know that we are beholden to serve Sir John, and Lady Middleton amidst their illustrious friends. Shall we desert them so precipitately in this, their hour of need?"

Margaret heard her mother's words with heavy heart. Lady Middleton's celebrations she knew all too well, the complement *and* the elaborate preparations. As for the Comtesse, she had, she could safely admit to herself, seen quite enough of the lady. If there were regret to her quitting the company, it was the missing of the most of her new friend, Lady Clara's visit. When might she ever encounter her like again? As for the others, what were they to her?

"*This*, Mama, against the joy of seeing Elinor and Marianne within the month?" cried she. "Surely your tenderest feelings must cry shame at the thought. Come, dearest Mama, do let us go, and soon, to see my sisters."

"But it is not only of Sir John that I think. Margaret, you must remember that I have at last engaged Master Jacob Frost to make improvements to our house. You know how long I have desired a drier roof and a more handsome staircase. I fear that I cannot leave that enterprise entirely in the hands of the servants."

"On the contrary, Mama," replied her daughter with a half-smile. "I *know* Hodges to be more equal to that task than either you or myself. Have you not observed how Master Frost quails under her eye?"

"Hodges does excellent well under *my* supervision," said her mother, "but she cannot be left without a steadying hand.

Yet I can see no reason," added she, "why *you*, my child, might not go ahead with Annie, while I remain here to look to our artisans—and assist with the hospitality at Barton—before joining all the family in just enough time for their entertainments at Delaford."

So, to the satisfaction of both it was arranged; Margaret, pleased to remove herself from the unsettling company of William du Plessy and her mother, having secured for herself, by virtue of her fancied efficiency, the opportunity to enjoy not one but two sets of festivities.

Part Two

8

Meanwhile, news of such import had reached Elinor that she could no longer consider her husband's musicians *or* their tribulations of much consequence. For the day before had brought a letter to Edward from his mother, Mrs. Henrietta Ferrars. The lady extraordinarily announced her intention to visit her son at Delaford Parsonage within the fortnight.

Edward received this news with some distress. Mrs. Ferrars had early made herself plain concerning her disappointment with her elder son's choice both of profession and wife, deeming the latter insufficiently dowered, and the former no less than a defection from family duty.

Having manifested her moral indignation by redisposing her inheritance in favor of Edward's younger brother Robert, she had maintained her righteous disapproval by limiting her come-at-ability to virtual estrangement. Until this, never had they expected to see her in Dorset.

''What can have possessed her?'' Edward said in some alarm. ''And why so urgent, after so long a neglect? My good mother, dear Elinor, seldom acts upon impulse; or most certainly, if ever she has done so, I have seen little of it. She must have reason. I cannot so much as divine this unheralded appearance on her part. What can have altered her view?'' he could but ask now.

Elinor—who had encountered the lady rarely, knew only what she *had seen* in her was an unassailable self-assurance in all matters, and what she *had heard* from her, a series of remarkable pronouncements—must still calm her sweet-natured husband, though it could be disputed whether even she entirely credited the suggestions which her wifely optimism now deemed proper.

''Do not upset yourself, my dear Edward,'' she began, ''for her inclinations could quite possibly turn out more agreeable than you surmise. She is your own mother still. Do remember, my love, that she grows older. Perhaps she yearns for reconciliation with her son. She need only see you well and happy to secure her certainty that you are not after all,'' and at this she looked up at her husband playfully, ''miserable in the too-modest calling you have chosen for yourself. We shall receive her with pleasure and hope that past differences might finally be forgotten.''

Edward shook his head dolefully at the unlikeliness of this prospect; but no matter, Elinor would hasten to make preparation. Provision for the arrival of such an exalted guest must commence immediately, her comfort seen to, that nothing might be lacking.

The Delaford Parsonage resembled in no way such accommodation as that to which Mrs. Ferrars was accustomed; yet, Elinor thought with satisfaction that their house was now become well-appointed, and she knew it to be well-situated. In these brilliant autumn days, just to look towards their opulent cedar and beyond that towards the vista of the hills with their display of color would be certain to please her guest. She rushed to ready the suite her own mother usually occupied when she did not rest with Marianne at Delaford.

Edward watched her arrangements with satisfaction and even, as the days passed, a lightening heart. His life, he began to feel, could fortunately no longer depend upon his mother's instability. Free at last of the burden of her caprice, he hoped now he might stir in her instead some admiration for his remarkable wife, even some respect for his accomplishment.

Nor did many days elapse after these quarters were scrubbed and freshened, clean linens provided, cushions puffed, before their new occupant's carriage could be heard entering the lane. Mrs. Ferrars' arrival, like the first wave of an unexpected storm, washed over the entire household. Every servant (though, in truth, there were few) was engaged by her. It was early evening; still the traveler would instantly to her repose. Mrs. Ferrars scarcely greeted her hosts before retiring to her quarters.

Elinor was nevertheless grateful. Now we have

seen her in, she thought to herself, all will be well again. Edward's spirits must be much lifted by this honor—and I more than contented—whatever may have occasioned her change of heart, to see his mother once again loving towards him.

The next morning, the lady rose late. It was near midday before she made an appearance among them and was ready for refreshment. If his mother's coming was meant to introduce Edward to any developments he had not anticipated, he had yet to learn of them. For the clergyman, who had returned hastily from his more urgent rounds, the wait continued arduous.

When she did descend, the elder Mrs. Ferrars seemed to her agitated son to have altered little with the years. She was a small woman but an elegant, despite an ochreous cast to her skin. Although not of height, she had always stood erect, as one whose back was even that instant being put up to a measure. Today especially her tiny frame expanded and seemed imposing—even tall—as she greeted her elder son's wife.

"You seem to have done well enough, Mrs. Ferrars," was her salutation upon a cursory inspection of the Parsonage, "in bringing to life a structure which could have provided little comfort to your predecessors." This assessment she apparently considered generous, even quite gracious. It enabled her to proceed without delay to the business that had brought her to her son's house.

Turning to him, "I am glad to see, Edward, that you have not permitted your modest means to bear *you* down to a way of life so far beneath that of the world our family has inhabited these many generations. I should be much aggrieved if such were your situation. The Ferrars are gentlemen; it behooves them to carry their heritage proudly, no matter the depth to which circumstances reduce them.''

With this she inclined towards him as if to impart a confidence, ''It is this very matter that I have journeyed to Dorset to take up with you. From just such consultations with your dear sister Fanny at Norland have I newly come,'' and diverted for a moment by the recollection, she smiled, adding with satisfaction, ''and I confess to it, I have never seen Mr. and Mrs. John Dashwood's properties more elegant. Their improvements upon the estate continue rigorous. I promise you, you will be speechless when next you visit.''

Elinor's consternation upon receiving this intelligence of her childhood home may only be guessed. Improvements to her beloved, stately Norland? Of what could they possibly consist?

''Is my brother then,'' began she as gently as she might, ''going forward with additions to that fine old house where I grew up?''

Mrs. Ferrars seemed surprised by the question, for Elinor's former intimacy with Norland had never so much as intruded upon her thoughts.

Then, recollecting herself, she explained, ''Ah, Mrs. Ferrars, I expect you will be pleased to learn that your brother John and my dear daughter together have at last engaged an architect suitable to transforming his father's properties. He is one

Richard Wyatt of London, fortunately at liberty after his late dispute with Lady Denton, an obstinate woman, as everyone knows. He has set to work immediately to remove those cumbersome wings from the structure and encased the main house delightfully in white plaster. Besides that, he has added two superb porticos and surrounded them with double Doric colonnades. It is a new edifice entirely; Norland's former self cannot be so much as detected. Our Fanny is enchanted by Wyatt's wizardry; she will soon enough see to the resurrection of the parklands as well. His ideas for *that*, as you may conceive, are boundless.''

Grave once more, the lady addressed her son. ''I have found myself concerned, dear Edward,'' said she, ''for the maintenance of our *own* endowments. Truth to tell, I fear for their future.''

Edward was bewildered by this statement. His mother, till this, had shown herself nothing but satisfied with the engagement of Robert for the preservation of their fortune. *He*, despite all, was his mother's favored son. His extravagance she had ever tolerated, nay, encouraged. His penchant for gambling was also not unknown to her. She had even, although reluctantly, embraced his improbable helpmeet, the former Lucy Steele.

''But dear mother,'' said he, ''surely my brother must see that our holdings are well looked to, as you have charged him?''

''I regret that I can no longer consent to agree to your judgment on this,'' responded the lady. ''Whatever good sense your brother may have displayed in the past must now be eclipsed by his profligacies, and those of his ambitious wife. I have no desire to burden you with more on this unfortunate matter, other than to say that I find myself obliged to think again concerning the threat to our family name.''

Still perplexed, Edward would learn more of what set her so stoutly against that which she had formerly considered secure; but his mother, it seemed, had delivered all she intended on the subject, and would continue in another vein.

''You will be pleased to learn,'' said she, ''that we are soon to be joined by your cousin, my sister Osborne's son George, so long in the West Indies. He is but now returned and eager to rekindle family feeling. He is often in my company, to my great delight.

''Dear George,'' continued she, ''is gifted with every grace; *his* person is noticed wherever he appears; mark you, he will make something of himself. My sister's son, I warrant, is to become a figure of whom any family may be proud. The pity of it is, he does not bear the Ferrars name''—and with a meaningful look—''yet a name is but a name, and that is easily amended after all.''

Edward and his wife listened astounded. Ever dutiful, he had always deferred to Mrs. Ferrars' decisions, whatever he may have thought of their wisdom. *He* could hardly question such baffling reversal. Could his mother indeed mean to unseat her younger son in favor of a new-found nephew?

He put aside these thoughts and, keeping his

countenance, hastened to assure her of their eagerness not only to welcome this relative but to introduce them to the agreeable society of their neighborhood.

"Dearest Mama," offered he, "you are well met, as will be my Osborne cousin too, for within the week we are to celebrate at a ball; it will be a festive evening honoring our own church musicians. I promise you it will be fully as joyous as any you have seen even while my father lived."

Elinor affixed her cordiality to her husband's invitation. Once again, her dear Edward's good sense made even this lady's petulance seem inconsequential. She was relieved to be permitted to serve her breakfast in tranquil silence.

9

While this exceptional familial reconciliation was taking place at Delaford Parsonage, a no less uplifting conversation was proceeding in Sussex at the home of Mrs. Ferrars' daughter Fanny and her husband John Dashwood. They, like Edward and Elinor, were pondering their mother's irresolution; but unlike that unsuspecting pair, *they* glimpsed in her vacillation an advantage.

Admirable was the dispatch with which this exemplary couple pursued such good fortune as was rightfully theirs. Since the death of his own respected father, John Dashwood had continued manfully coping with the generous inheritance into which he had come. Having dutifully established himself as master of his father's neglected estate and house, he immediately set about to elevate his situation. Through his enclosure of the Norland common and altruistic acquisition of the adjoining farms, lest they fall into other hands—by all his tireless replanning and refurbishing, he had put the munificent legacy to fine account.

How fortunate had he been in his good lady during those trying times. John Dashwood's benevolent character was such as would have ruined him in the face of the incessant demands by his dear mother and sisters. Were it not for the fortitude and vigilance of his Fanny, there might have been no predicting the conclusion.

"Why, dearest John," she often reminded him, "I shall not forget how our many kindnesses to those ladies then went unnoted. How ill Mrs. Dashwood took my every attempt, after your father's untimely death, to make herself and her daughters welcome here in this, their former home. Why, upon one occasion, I well recall, I was upon the point of bringing forward for them our second-best silver. I assure you, I did contemplate it. And to what end! Your mother, you must remember, took herself off to Devonshire with the best of your uncle's possessions. What could *she* have wanted with our elegant chairs, our carved tables! And consider the china and the linens, ah, dearest John! On such a scant income, how could such fine furnishings concern her *or* her daughters? I can only think a monstrous greed overtook her. Why, Norland was a mere shadow of itself after they left. To consider so little her husband's own home, and it the very place that all her girls had loved so well? Unheard of!"

It was certainly true—and any visitor to the Sussex estate might attest to this miracle of restoration—that with unflagging energy, Fanny Dash-wood had arranged for the replacement of all the missing belongings. She had seen to it that *her* Nor-land could be found lacking in few elegant accoun-trements, or any comforts to be found in the best houses. Yet the recollection of those first months, amidst her husband's uncompanionable relatives—most particularly would she remember Mrs. Dash-wood's unyielding daughters—would linger long with the new mistress of Norland.

More exasperating was what was yet to befall poor Fanny—and this new injury from no less a source than her own family. Scrupulous had she ever been in her filial attention to Mrs. Ferrars—according to that lady's every whim the full con-sideration of both a daughter's duties and the hope of a generous settlement—all to no avail. Instead, she discovered that despite her dedicated ministra-tions, when Mrs. Ferrars considered a change in her estate—the transfer of her fortune from Edward to Robert—her daughter Fanny had counted for naught.

Nor had she, as compliant offspring, other choice. Fanny must accept her mother's superior judgment in the matter; however, she would voice her doubtful assessment of it to her own dear hus-band.

"Of course," she was wont to say, "I know my mother to be the most affectionate parent in the world; to be sure, she needs must be firm with my brother Edward. His choice of profession was dis-tasteful; but by far his worse offense was his choice

in your haughty sister Elinor. After all that had
passed between us, how could he embrace such a
woman? So shameful a neglect of family wishes by
an elder son could not go unaccounted. When he
announced his intentions there, I too applauded my
mother's anger, heartily so! But alas,'' she would
continue, sighing, ''I must amend as well that in
her choice of an alternative beneficiary, she could
hardly be expected to have elicited my approval.
Dashing figure he may be, but my brother Robert
can never meet our great family's expectation. I
think it a pity that she can not entertain a more
suitable heir. Our son Harry, for instance, who coos
at her so agreeably. Yet she does not consider him.
I confess, I fear the consequences.''

Now Fanny Dashwood glimpsed the reward of
patience. A woman not easily discouraged in pur-
poses near to her heart, she had never abandoned
hope for her young son. Whatever she may have
felt, she had kept Mrs. Ferrars' good will; a dedicated daughter, she had reflected, must continue to
support her mother, no matter how foolish or ill-
advised her enterprises. Having at last discovered
the impossibility of her choice of Robert, the elder
lady was left for the time being without heir.

''Think of our little one,'' said Fanny, newly
hopeful. ''Surely, now she has finally come to her
senses, my mother must consider a loving grand-
child before all others.''

With characteristic charity, Fanny Dashwood
would not allow her plan for her son to interfere
with the cultivation of her burgeoning friendship

with Mrs. Robert Ferrars. When the presumed successors to the Ferrars estate would make their visits from London, Fanny had seen to it that they were included in the many lavish entertainments in progress at Norland. She had done so at first from prudence of self-interest, but swiftly discovered a recompense for her diligence. She found in her new sister-in-law a companion gratifying to her taste.

Lucy Ferrars brought into her view another world. Her country relative eagerly attended to every fashionable nuance and studied the brisk London manners of her new relation. In Lucy, Fanny saw a smartness she admired, even coveted. Lucy's quick eye, clipped delivery, gaiety—her superior knowledge of the world, in short—enticed.

Best of all in the eyes of Mrs. Dashwood was her new sister's fine discrimination in recognizing the outstanding quality of her son, Harry Dashwood. Of the former Lucy Steele's rapturous appreciation of children, we have already seen much made. And of her new-found nephew, she declared him, "all enchantment," and doted upon his every action.

"How well is he formed, so tall he has outgrown by a head his Middleton cousin," she observed often, always within the child's hearing. "Surely the dear boy resembles his well-favored family. Does he not liken to my sweet husband?" Then, addressing herself to the nine-year-old, she would coax him towards an inspiring future.

"You too, dear Harry, must be sure to grow into

a man of fashion and just like your fine uncle Robert, surpassing any about you in elegance.''

Such an inspiring prospect suited the boy. He strutted about like a peacock. His mother's response equaled his own. Towards her new relation, her demeanor was warmth itself.

Mutual adulation fostered intimacy; the two soon became a pair. Even happier for both as they saw more of one another, their conversation ranged increasingly. More nourishing even than the continual praise for her son was the pleasure to be taken in decrying the shortcomings of Elinor Ferrars, thus securing the bond between these natural confidantes. Edward's choice of wife provided an arena in which they vied as to which had discerned earlier the deficiencies of their common sister-in-law.

''From the very instant, dear Fanny, that I encountered Elinor Dashwood at Lady Middleton's, accompanied by her sister Marianne,'' began Lucy on one occasion, ''I was staggered by her reserve, and her sister's arrogance. More striking was the coldness of both towards the children—those four irresistible Middleton darlings. And how might *I* have ignored that indifference? Such is the warmth of my own nature that I comprehend it not at all.''

With this assessment Fanny Dashwood could hardly agree more emphatically. ''It does not startle me,'' she asserted, ''for I myself could not please them, though for the sake of my dear husband I tried. If you were acquainted with their mother as I have been, you might come to understand her daughters.''

Lucy Ferrars charitably conceded that for her part she might overlook their faults, had there been any hint of stylishness about them. "They set themselves far above both Mrs. Jennings and myself, and yet have no understanding of the greater world. And always there is that certainty that they alone are capable of refinement. Now I can only wonder at myself for not having seen more clearly how little I required acquaintance with those ladies." Her own thoughts here must include Edward; but of her former attachment to *him* she thought it better not to speak.

From this, the two progressed to a consideration of their mother's, Mrs. Ferrars' fickleness. Such plaints enlivened their daily round.

As for Mr. Robert Ferrars, his excursions into the country were less extended. He was a man heavily weighted with duty. There was first his preoccupation with trips to the London shops in quest of modish attire. Always had he been impeccable, but his elevation to heir, he understood, had made such attention to his person the more necessary.

In view of these grand prospects, he had been obliged to cast his lot with the best young men about town, a number of glittering, boisterous fellows dedicated to sport, above all to boxing, whose demands were more exacting than any he had formerly known. To be worthy of such exalted company must imply a fidelity to the latest fashion. Robert Ferrars had, for example, recently felt himself impelled to swagger about in vast swathes of neckcloth. He had even cropped his hair after the guise of the pugilists, so much did he admire them.

Even greater demands were there upon him in keeping abreast of boxing matches, not only in London but in the countryside. Any pugilistic encounter, in truth, whatever knock-down fight with bare fists took place, became a sporting event to meditate upon. So it was that every day of the week, he awoke to heavy responsibilities. From the first minute of the morning until the last at night, he must ponder the laying of his bets.

When the business of his mother's estate would intrude, it impinged upon his commitments. Time, he discovered, was too short for matters of such scant import to him. As for his lively new wife, he was delighted that Lucy had found such good company in his sister at Norland. Mrs. Ferrars, at least, made no objection when he set out for London on his own to his boxing, the cricket matches, or to his gaming clubs.

On the contrary, Lucy delighted in her dapper husband's new passion. She admired his associates, people of some importance with virtually unlimited money and continuing leisure. Herself immediately noticed by several of these gallants when they called to take her husband from her, she felt satisfaction in her improved social position since marrying. Before long she must, of course, boast of such recognition to his sister, closeted so far away in the country.

"You should be astonished at how these gentlemen and their ladies do talk, dearest Fanny," said she. "You might sometimes think that an encounter between two such noted champions were a national debate, to hear them carry on. Robert and all his elegant friends are, I assure you, positively bewitched by the sport! They seem never to get enough. The silliest nonsense you can imagine just occurred in the late battle of the pugilists on Lowfield Common near Crawley. To hear your dear brother's retelling is most engaging. The championship so favored Boyce over Dutch Sam that there was little danger of loss. Then, of a sudden, the stakes were much in contention. Can you picture it, sister, the umpires entertained different opinions? Some nonsense regarding a blow to the knees as foul. And they themselves quarreling wildly when the trouble started. There was pandemonium, and no settling the match. Robert and his companions are in arms over such shilly-shallying judges, the foolish delays, and the 'no payments' for who knows how long. Have you ever heard the like? Is it not too diverting?"

Fanny Dashwood was brought to attention by this last. She listened enrapt, would inquire further into the extent of her brother's losses and, more particularly, into his commitment of his mother's assets during the exchange.

Lucy gaily confided all she heard to her sympathetic sister. "You know how clever our Robert is, how resourceful. Why, you may be assured, dearest Fanny, that he has already turned his losses around at the gaming table to make up the sums."

Her sister-in-law, if alarmed, revealed nothing. She saw that she must bide her time.

10

Marianne's artless greeting, together with the exhilaration Margaret experienced journeying so distant from her humdrum chores at Barton Park, brought our young lady to Dorset in the highest of spirits. Moreover, Mrs. Brandon's pleasure in seeing her little sister so lighthearted could not but bring merriment. For in truth, the change in Margaret since her sister's departure was marked.

"Margaret, can it really be you?" exclaimed Marianne, "the raggedy, wind-blown silly who excelled in tangling her stitchery, whose gown was ever muddied? Why, in such finery I can hardly make you out. With your pelisse, and your bonnet tied so to perfection."

"Well, now, this is praise indeed from the fine Mrs. Brandon," returned Margaret, smiling. "Might I venture, poor bumpkin as I am, to observe in turn how admirably matrimony sits upon the mistress of Delaford?"

Such was their delight in their reunion that they

talked animatedly for near an hour, until Elinor was able to come to them. Their eldest sister had hastened to Delaford as quickly as she might. Immediately she greeted her, she too must allow for Margaret's emergence.

"Why, dear girl, what complexion you are in, and how your eyes do shine. Has she not, Marianne, become quite splendid? You must tell us everything of sweet Mama and our Devonshire friends. Can our mother really have chosen this season to embark upon her cherished improvements?"

Elinor was eager to join in her sisters' mirth but, beleaguered as she was by the presence of the elder Mrs. Ferrars, could barely contrive it. Dutiful, she would yet inquire after the news of their former abode, urging Margaret to tell them everything of her life there, now she and Marianne were no longer a part of it. And patient as ever, she would listen to her sister's recital.

Margaret was no stranger to apprehension in Elinor, who—or so it had seemed to her—was always under the weight of the family's responsibilities. So this playful member of the family chose instead to take pity on her sister and attempt to divert her. It had been Margaret's practice to relieve her sisters in their difficult moments by embellishing whatever frivolous news she had come upon. Today, to entertain them, she rehearsed her current repertoire—the freshest doings of their neighbors, the indomitable Middletons, in their efforts to forge links to important society.

"You will hardly credit it, dear ladies," she began with an impish air, "but we in Devonshire can lately boast of our most exalted associations. I assure you, you shall find no more stylishness at Brighton, or even at Court itself. For *we* now move in the height of fashion. *None* surpass us. Why, *notre couture,*" and at this, she pranced about and fluttered her gown and slippers, "is more *à la mode* even than your very own here in Dorset."

Marianne, enlivened by this exhibition, laughed and demanded more particulars regarding their evenings. The youngest sister performed with verve.

She depicted Mrs. Jennings' stately school friends. First, the charming, wise Lady Clara Ashburton in her patient attempts to improve the Middleton offspring; and next the entrance of Madame la Comtesse Isabel du Plessy in Parisian *grandeur,* and her condescension in all things. And the while," Margaret smilingly reassured them, "dear Sir John simply agog with admiration.

"Better still, is what follows," she went on, "an unpredicted appearance of that lady's ever-so-dashing son, Mr. William du Plessy. A young lieutenant of such agreeable nature that compliments flow from him, I vow, like honey from the comb."

How might not this intelligence command vigorous attention from Marianne, who remained unregenerate when romance was potential?

"But tell us more, dearest Margaret," she urged, "of this remarkable young man. What sort is he? Surely you can not think him so like his officious mother that you will not so much as entertain his amusing you of an evening?"

"Whether he be or no," said Margaret, now serious, "I cannot fathom. The difference in *his* demeanor from any of our own is prodigious; between us, in truth, there seemed a chasm. He is so very Continental, you see, as is his proud mother. Indeed, *she* deplores the very idea of English address. She speaks of our manner—and all of us as well—as aloof, impassive, even lacking inspiration. I fear we are quite unappealing to her. La Comtesse endlessly laments the loss of her associates in a city that was civilization itself. A born Englishwoman, she yet found Paris her life."

"I do lament for the dear lady," mused Marianne, affected, "having known such glowing society, to be thus deprived." Then, recovering her animation and looking at Margaret mischievously, "And in the company of such as Sir John and his lady—indeed all the good Middletons—or even of their kindly if maladroit mother, how would she not mourn? To be so humbled, the poor creature! Why, I myself could bear their society very little. Consider how often *I* would run from it."

At this, Elinor bid the pair check themselves. "Marianne, how can you?" she intervened. "When Mrs. Jennings was like a mother to us in the most arduous circumstances!"

Properly chastened, the younger sisters shared a smile. Margaret spoke instead of the only one of that company who suited her entirely. She told them of her explorations into the countryside with Lady Clara, of their intimate conversation, and of how she had inspired her to devote herself anew to her drawing.

"Lady Clara possesses her own tranquillity," Margaret explained. "She opens my eyes to nature as I have never imagined it before."

"How it delights me to hear of this worthy new companion," cried Elinor. "And what good fortune that the lady takes pleasure in the very pursuits you most enjoy. I can remember our own never-ending quest for such discoveries. Ah, Marianne, was it not so? Sweet were our walks out to the wildness of those vistas. But, lovely child," she said, hugging Margaret, "now so grown that I hardly know you, your sister and I have fretted over just such a lack of discerning company. And we so far away. Mama's recountings of liveliness admist the Middletons, of course, we read in her every letter; but it is more reassuring by far to hear of contentment from yourself."

Not for the world would Margaret disabuse her good sister as to her often restless state of mind in that generally inferior society. She preferred to continue just as gaily as they had begun. And laughing, she responded with, "Yet dear Elinor, I do willingly confess that I am ready to abandon Barton's finest blessings in favor of your kind invitation. I own that I look to the ball at Delaford House with some excitement. To be exact, I expect wonders from it. I have little doubt that we shall be enchanted."

In the last weeks, Mrs. Brandon had indeed been

venturesome, and she assured her sister that her undertaking had occupied all of her energies.

"You must understand, dear Margaret, that to begin with, just to smooth the affairs of our battling musicians took some artifice. They required daily, even hourly, encomia to ensure their cooperation. And only minutes ago, sisters, I explained to these gentlemen—how all the county will be in their tender care, how the music must be equal even to their glorious church performance—if somewhat lighter-hearted and even a little frivolous, how I depended upon their artistry—how I knew *that* to be of the highest from my brother Ferrars, and how they alone might make the occasion the most talked-about that any in Delaford have ever attended. Ah, the patience it took. My dears, you may depend upon it—we shall now have them as our slaves for the evening."

Nor had Marianne's dedication ended with winning over the wayward musicians. She had also taken advantage of this festivity to mend a hurt to her husband, which she knew he had been suffering for too long. John Edgerton of Atherton Hall—a most worthy gentleman of an eminent county family—lived quietly with his wife and daughter at a comfortable distance from Delaford; yet in all her time in Dorset, Marianne had only heard them spoken of. It would seem that Edgerton had fallen out with the Colonel's father while he lived, and although Marianne knew not why, the families remained estranged. Marianne, seeing her husband's regret over the rift, and too sensible of his earlier sadness, had determined to restore to him his childhood neighbors.

Her invitation to the Edgertons having been accepted with alacrity, she already felt certain she had achieved much. Encouraged by this success—along with her confidence in the supremacy of her cook's hot soup with negus—she was straightaway able to turn her attention to that most requisite duty of any hostess: ensuring for her young lady guests a quantity of young men for dancing.

"I am satisfied that there can be no ball with too many gentlemen," was her judgment. "And for this occasion I have seen to this matter admirably, dear Margaret, if only for your sake. Still, to look upon you, I expect you would be very much in request these days, whether there be many partners or no. And I give you leave, if you dare it, to lose your heart to any or even all of these gallants, if you so choose. On this evening, your charge will be to bask in your consequence, and more pertinent, to be admired as you savor the pleasures of the dance."

When the day came, amid the bustle there was thus the certainty that few could object to the exertions so admirably invested by Mrs. Brandon. The Colonel stood by proudly in his evening attire, himself a man to be envied. He contemplated his wife, her lately arrived Mama and younger sister at her side, while she greeted her many guests, their names coming comfortably to her tongue in her salutations. And at the smiles of approval for everything she said or did, he grew exultant.

Among their first guests were the Ferrars, of course, these now accompanied by Edward's mother, and with her an unknown young gentleman. Marianne, who had encountered the lady but once, remembered her little, and what she did recall of her was hardly of the most pleasant. Yet for the sake of her sister Mrs. Brandon would make every attempt to greet her warmly and assure her of a proper welcome at Delaford.

The elder Mrs. Ferrars, to the contrary, made a more valiant endeavor. She recollected their earlier acquaintance in Harley Street long ago. "I delight, Madam," said she with her customary graciousness, "to see how you have improved in circumstance during the late years. When last we met, I observed you reduced and pale. Was not your health at that time imperiled by some affair of the heart?"

Observing her hostess redden, she relented. "But," said she, "perhaps I mistake you for one of your sisters—you have them, I believe. No matter, dear Madam since I find you now restored and—fancy it!—mistress of a fine estate."

Marianne, in deference to her solemn oath to Elinor, ignored this. Instead, the hostess turned the lady's attention to the more pleasing sight of the happy couple before her. She spoke first of her own dear husband's astonishment at the remarkable transformation of the parish under young Ferrars' supervision.

"Dear Madam, the influences of your ingenious son, Parson Ferrars, are everywhere you look in our community. Why only lately did he work a miracle, when he proposed larger garden plots for tilling. My dear Colonel is full of gratitude, for not only are the cottagers enriched, but so as well is the capital value of the benefice. How you are to be commended for having fostered talents such as his.''

Mrs. Ferrars turned aside with impatience towards the gentleman accompanying her. In presenting *him* to her hosts, her manners were improved appreciably. "Though I regard your assessment of my son, Mrs. Brandon, it is my nephew here," said she, "for whom I may claim true distinction. Not only has he been seen, and made his remarkable way into distant parts of the world, but before long, I trust, we shall be privileged to witness his welcome into Parliament.''

Mr. George Osborne was but of medium stature, yet held himself extraordinarily well. He was groomed exquisitely in the fashion of London. His address, if clipped, was proper, and he appeared a pleasant young man who knew when to listen, when to be silent, and better, to be brief when he spoke.

"You are too good, Mrs. Brandon, to welcome me, a stranger, and on such a festive occasion. My aunt had given me to believe that I should find your Delaford company congenial. She was wrong; everything here that I see is of fascination.''

While addressing his hostess, his gaze moved towards the young lady standing at Mrs. Brandon's side. It was a look that said a great deal.

Presentations made, the young man had scarcely time to engage Margaret for an early dance when he was recovered by his sponsor, who wore an expression of displeasure. Plainly, *she* required his devotion every moment and would allow no disregard. Reluctant did he turn from his new acquaintances and resume his station. The pair moved smartly off in the direction of the Colonel, for Mrs. Ferrars deemed it proper that *she* and her nephew converse only with the master of Delaford, not those whom his wife had seen fit to gather in from the countryside for the evening's gala.

So it was that Margaret saw little of this gentleman until he claimed his turn to dance. Without Mrs. Ferrars by his side, his demeanor she found was altered perceptibly, as was his manner of address.

"Your sister, Mrs. Brandon," began he in studied tones and as though pronouncing an eulogy, "is much to be commended. To do such hospitable work in the course of her many responsibilities, especially in the service of my cousin Edward, is charitable. Though I confess that I have seldom attended such an occasion, I am honored to present myself at the behest of my aunt."

"But, Sir," responded Margaret laughing, "do you then reserve your favor for your intimates alone? And do you not fancy the gaiety of a ballroom? The music is sweet, the dancers lively— what more might there be to wish for of an evening? You yourself seem easy in its surroundings."

"Do I then appear to you so, Miss Dashwood? Were you but to survey your own happy situation this evening—at home with both sisters and your mother—and then consider and give a thought to my own, you might not think so. Ah, what a wonder is a close family! How it does provide for secure society wherever we may be. You are fortunate in the tenderness about you.''

''Are you then yourself, Sir,'' said Margaret startled, ''without living parents, brother or sister? That is melancholy. Yet you have your aunt's devotion, which must count for much.''

''Our acquaintance is but new,'' said he, ''for I grew to manhood in the West Indies, my father's only son, a solitary youth, and orphaned early. Miss Dashwood, I envy the affection I see in every family. My own father was a man as unsocial as he was short-lived, and I a stranger to my aunt and cousins. Yet I am determined to know, to enjoy them in time, to join them, to share their comforts. I too long for family.''

The gentleman was most earnest, his frankness appealing, his situation of the most touching.

''But I impose with my sorrows, Miss Dashwood,'' said he then, ''when my wish is only to engage.''

Margaret nodded acknowledgment, and they danced together in contentment for the remainder of the set.

11

⚬⚬⚬⚬⚬⚬

In that part of Dorset—a district acclaimed for its sociality by those happy enough to reside there—all could be secure of sedulous regard. For its more genteel families, there was never coldness or indifference to any news of well- or ill-being. Delaford was of just that comfortable size to include frequent encounters with familiars while idling in the few shops of the town. It allowed for the most cordial daily visits, for supping at leisure, and dances of an evening. Withal it must needs be avowed that the neighborhood, like many another welcoming township, was not altogether free of the less amiable impertinence of curiosity. As a consequence, pryers, tattlers, and gossips were seldom in short supply.

The occasion of the ball at Delaford House provided potential for even the most demanding of that expectant company. Not only was there the certain joy of scrutinizing the country's newest visitors and pronouncing unhindered upon their dress and de-

meanor, but the prospect of the Edgertons' attendance promised titillation, embarrassment, and perhaps some discomposure on the part of their hosts.

Thus, when Mr. John Edgerton, with his wife and
their daughter, was announced among the assembled many that night at the Brandons', a palpable
hush descended upon the room, its gaiety silenced.
Up to that moment, Mrs. Brandon had cheerfully
engaged with the continuing stream of ladies and
gentlemen appearing, until of a sudden she too noticed the alteration and turned eagerly towards her
new arrivals. The stillness was as sharp as one commanded by the rap of a baton, and that the more
notable as it was soon followed by persistent whispering.

John Edgerton, an imposing gentleman of mature
years, had entered looking strained, and was seen
to be searching out his host.

As the Colonel moved towards them, the entire
company seemed to wait uncertain of what might
be witnessed in the confrontation between the two
long-estranged neighbors.

Alas for those souls that would revel in the woes
of others. A reticent if heartfelt handshake was exchanged between the older gentleman and his host.

Mr. Edgerton spoke first. ''The years since I last
set foot in this house are many; they have worn
heavily upon us all. Indeed, I should hardly have
imagined it possible to behold you, the younger of
Henry Brandon's sons—and the very one kept at
such a distance by his own father—so properly in-

stalled as heir to Delaford. I bring you, if belatedly, my salutations.''

Colonel Brandon was moved by the generosity of his address. "Good Sir," was his response, "I cannot express my own feelings of warmth towards yourself and your dear family. Given what you have suffered at the hands of mine, I should expect nothing. In truth, I believed *I* had lost my good friends altogether." Hesitating, then leading them towards his wife, he continued, "I hope we may soon enough, whilst we are more in private, open our hearts to one another as well as to our sad past; but for now, my dearest Mrs. Brandon awaits your company, and with such an eagerness that I dare not detain her a moment longer."

Mr. Edgerton sighed and seemed relieved. All grace, he brought forward his family towards Mrs. Brandon. And it was not long after that the little group were chatting amiably.

"Dear Mrs. Edgerton," said Marianne, "allow me to present to you my own mother, as well as my sister Margaret, the youngest of us, this evening so happily attending."

Mrs. Dashwood was promptness itself in undertaking to look to the older of the ladies, who was infirm and had already stood too long, leading her towards a sofa where they could sit in comfort for their converse.

As Colonel Brandon moved with Mr. Edgerton to join their neighbors, Marianne and Margaret sought to make his daughter easy. Yet Miss Letitia Edgerton remained solemn, offering no more than formal courtesy. She was a thin lady, something wan, the sadness of whose features confirmed keen disappointment. Still, to look upon her, it could be surmised that she had once been fair of aspect.

As was her wont, Marianne could not rest until she had done her utmost to urge this lady to enter in the pleasure of the hour. At the very least, she thought, it should content her to see her father recover a friendship once so valued by him.

"Miss Edgerton, I know you will rejoice with me to find amity between our families after so long. Though I myself know little of the nature of their disagreement, in all candor I take delight in seeing my husband rejoice over the possibility of harmony restored. Neighbors we are, after all, and should be ready to serve one another as need occurs."

"You are kind," was Miss Edgerton's response. "My memories of this house come rushing forward, and many are of the happiest, I will own." She broke off, appearing too moved to continue.

Marianne could see her discomfort, and would not wish to disturb her further. Yet after a time, Miss Edgerton recovered her calm and herself chose to resume. "I did spend many days of my youth in this very room and in the company of my most valued friends, Mrs. Brandon; I confess to having seen it never looking more festive. You are to be congratulated. Yours are plainly happier hands in the management of Delaford."

Margaret, who had remained silent until this, hoped to enliven her guest with superlatives regarding her sister's enterprise.

"I assure you, Miss Edgerton, my sister is of that species who *can* work miracles, especially when she gives her mind to them."

At this, the lady brightened, and said laughing, "If only to look upon your brother, Miss Dashwood, I could believe easily in Mrs. Brandon's supernal powers. Never have I seen John Brandon as spirited, or as handsome—and I have known him since his earliest years. She must indeed be divinely capable, to have restored *him* so to his former self." She grew pensive as she recollected, "My dearest childhood friend, you see, was Eliza, his father's ward; we were inseparable as young girls. Your own husband, Mrs. Brandon, and his elder brother James were our constant companions." She fell silent again.

Marianne and Margaret, scarce comprehending the cause of Miss Edgerton's sorrow, inclined their heads. Yet could they have been listening to the murmurs in the room, what a doleful a story might they have heard. At that very moment, and in another corner, the Brandon's closest neighbors, Lord and Lady Brunton, were energetically rehearsing to Lady Brunton's young niece Harriet the sad history of Miss Letitia Edgerton.

"To look upon her today," that good lady was saying, "you would think she had never known the more tender feelings. Yet in her youth, she was ever as devoted to Colonel Brandon's elder brother James as young John loved Eliza Williams, his father's ward. But since old Brandon deemed Letitia's dowry insufficiently ample—not near as grand a fortune to bring to his heir's marriage as was Eliza's—he would have none of the young people's desire. With his ward's fortune in prospect for the estate—and a sizable sum it was—why might he consider such frivolous variations as the young people themselves proposed? No indeed—he was a gentleman whose patience was short with any matter so foolish as the heart. No sooner had he observed the situation than he banished his younger son John from the household, sent him packing off to Sumatra or some other foreign shore. He then separated the girls, and simply forbade his elder son James to utter so much as a word to the Edgerton girl. The feckless lad obeyed, and there in poor Miss Letitia do we see the abject consequence."

"My dear Lady," reproved her husband, "surely you are too severe. As master of his estate, how could the gentleman not perform his duty? Much fortune was entailed, and none can fault keen attention to the preservation of property for the generations to come. Our friend was, as you observe, perhaps something stern; but think upon it, mere pups falling in love! Are we to honor such whims? Why, if we are to allow our young people to determine what is their own best course, who can tell where it may end? No, my dear one, he acted as any one of us would. He did his duty."

"Ah yes, to be sure, my love," cried his wife, "yet what suffering ensued. Lovely Eliza Williams' own dear parents had left her tenderly in their friend's trust. And the shame it brought to the Brandons, the scandal. No, good sir, talk not to me of duty. And *that* poor lady!'' Here Lady Brunton nodded towards Miss Edgerton, and added with no less emotion, ''No, my dear sir, old Henry Brandon made ruination of their lives.'' And looking to her attentive niece, she reminded her sternly, ''Which is not to suggest, my dear Harriet, that *you* may presume to regard your elders with anything but respect.''

Neither Mrs. Brandon nor her sister heard a word of this exchange; the ladies were instead assiduous in their attempt to divert their own conversation *from* the past.

''Is there a felicity in the world superior to this country in the autumn?'' was Mrs. Brandon's query engaging her guest, followed by her own rhapsodic refrain, ''A symphony of dead leaves in flight under its lowering sky. Oh, happy place! Happier we, to inhabit it.''

Miss Edgerton, though grateful to her hostess for her effort to inspire, remained dejected, and could not be prevailed upon to applaud that poetic vision of nature.

''I regret to confess it, but these many years I have noted such wonders in none of the seasons. In autumn, especially, more affecting to me are its dark skies and cutting winds, those ominous signs of the winter soon to descend upon us. For it is then that the loneliness of the days are so much felt. Still,'' she added, ''it is during the fiercest weather that I can be of service and make myself useful in the neighborhood. So many remain little cared for. For years, I have gone as far as Brighton, hoping to make a difference to the days of a desperate friend,'' explained she.

Marianne listened with a new attention and some perturbation. Though she dare not ask, she felt certain she comprehended the nature of Miss Edgerton's visits in Brighton. They must concern the welfare of the daughter of Eliza Williams, her childhood companion, and her natural son.

''How good you are, Miss Edgerton,'' was what she managed. ''I myself should be grateful for the chance to accompany you. Though my husband does not, I believe, favor my intervention, I could, I know, be of use to you.''

Margaret observed her sister's intensity, but before she could learn this lady's response, she was claimed by her spoken partner to join in the longaway just commencing. The music had continued lively, and the young man who appeared before her was ready. She decided to enjoy herself without further distraction. And as she progressed down the line, she was intercepted by George Osborne, whose melancholy visage cheered her the more.

Not to lose the instant's opportunity, he mumbled in an almost inaudible voice a question—Was it possible, might he, could he call upon her on the morrow? She found this awkwardness amusing, and rejoined that indeed he might—were he able to spare a moment from his exacting ''companion'' of the evening, Mrs. Ferrars, who seemed to strain to overhear their brief exchange.

12

Such extravagant dedication to her nephew on the part of Mrs. Ferrars could hardly go unobserved by her chosen heir *or* his wife. Robert and Lucy Ferrars had already remarked upon it. So much so that they too now deemed a journey to Dorset consequential.

A letter to that intent was received by Edward Ferrars the very day after the ball, informing the startled clergyman—who had not heard from his brother for a twelve-month and more—of the impending visit of yet others of his family. His younger brother wrote:

> *My dear Edward, We hear praise for your accomplishments, and not merely from those who mean to gain my good will or flatter our family's name. Therefore, brother, we come soon to pay our respects, which, I must confess, I believe to be in arrears. Lucy and I hope you will welcome us in the loving spirit we*

*now embrace you. We know your quarters to
be modest, and with our mother currently in
residence there, we have chosen instead to
lodge at an inn nearby, where our cousin Osborne is installed, and where we can be better
assured of commodiousness. We arrive Thurs-
day next.*

Yours,

Need it be said how this short missive struck our
harried parson and his good wife? While he found
himself perplexed, virtually struck dumb by these
developments, Elinor, so regularly a pillar of
strength in adversity, could be seen to be shaken by
the thought of close intercourse with the former
Lucy Steele.

The wearing mien of his mother and her retinue,
the unstated demands upon Edward, the perpetual
question of just what the lady's true wishes were
pertaining to her eldest, continued, in short, to disturb and vex.

"Dearest Edward," began Elinor, "whatever the
matter in their minds, we shall dispatch it; and the
while, we can greet your brother and sister with
cordiality and good cheer. You shall see."

Edward was silent, struggling to keep his customary evenness of temper. Composing himself as
best he could, he spoke. "My brother's sudden admiration, indeed the convergence upon us of so
many of my good family all at once, must have
some greater design, some special purpose. Their

good will, offered so improvidently, is I fear more ominous to me than joyous.''

Elinor, who understood what propelled their exertions, refrained from uttering her thoughts. It struck her that her husband's relatives were nothing if not covetous. She questioned what might their machinations have to do with Edward? *He* had early withdrawn from such struggle, sacrificing every claim upon the Ferrars' fortune. Justice alone demanded that he now be exempt from their contentions.

''Edward,'' she replied, ''they mean to make peace where earlier was none possible. Surely it is time for reconciliation, my love?''

Curious it was that when the elder Mrs. Ferrars learned of his brother's magnanimous communication, she greeted this intelligence with indifference.

''Your brother Robert has much to learn,'' she said, ''and we shall make it our business to see that he does. Even a passing acquaintance with his cousin Osborne could lead him to comprehension. Ours is an heralded name. Its heir must be equal to it.''

In this matter of deportment, Mrs. Ferrars knew whereof she spoke—exactly what was, and was *not*, acceptable. When later that day she went to call upon the Colonel and Mrs. Brandon, she demonstrated her command. Upon the arm of her nephew, whom she continued unwilling to spare, she made her appearance with the air of one conducting a state visit. Indeed, from the moment the lady and her escort were announced, the Colonel and his

wife must honor their wishes as they might the
Royal party itself. They made their condescension
felt and before the pair departed not an hour later,
had awed their hosts by their presence.

Mrs. Ferrars informed them that, having already
seen quite enough of their house, she would set
forth directly to scrutinize the Brandon properties.
She assembled her group, and they must follow in
train. Mr. Osborne comported himself admirably in
his aunt's eyes—by never leaving her side.

So commenced their inspection of the grape ar-
bor, the brewery, the stables, the parklands. Mrs.
Ferrars' questions concerning the estate and its
maintenance were so admirably exacting that
some—it must be conceded—could have seen them
intrusive. She would know each particular pertinent
to the security of her son's living.

"There can be little doubt, my dear Colonel, now
I have assessed it, that your father did well by
you," was her conclusion. "You seem to have an
ample estate at your disposal—a goodly stable,
your fields tilled, your cottages standing, your farmers biddable and devoted to their Church. I freely
commend you upon your sturdy management."

Margaret, who had dutifully made one of this
party, was entirely content to observe Mrs. Ferrars'
inspection. How diverting she found it just to accompany them. George Osborne, who on occasion
dared to glance her way, shrugged and seemed
something abstracted. That he was disappointed in
the morning's visit was clear enough; but his determination to gratify his aunt remained unshakable.

Family feeling, as he had asseverated to Miss Dash-wood, was foremost in his mind; *nothing* could deter him from devotion to it.

It was only the moment before their departure, while Mrs. Ferrars was making her adieus to the Brandons, that the young man detached himself long enough to lean in Margaret's direction and whisper, "I have today hardly paid the call I so eagerly sought, and you so cordially allowed. But ah, Miss Dashwood, please be assured that my thoughts were with you, though we have not perhaps this morning exchanged a word. Might I hope to spend a quiet hour in your presence some time soon?"—here glancing at his aunt—"although I confess to its unlikelihood in Dorset. Should it mean voyaging as far as Devonshire to do so, I would willingly undertake the journey; that is, if you are yet good enough to encourage it?"

Such a confidence, delivered with so doleful an expression could but interest Margaret. The very stealthiness of his tone, especially as it violated the discipline imposed by his aunt upon the entire company, piqued her. And in candor, she was flattered. She had scarcely considered how to offer encouragement before the formidable lady whisked her companion away.

Of one thing, she now judged, there could be little doubt. Mr. George Osborne kept fast in his attentions. Even so, his address appeared to Margaret almost comical, so without art was it. Poor gentleman, so well-meaning yet so inept.

Moreover, he proved scrupulously accurate in his

assessment of the continuing round of his Dorset engagements during the next days. His aunt claimed him entirely, and he was to see Miss Dashwood very little.

Diversion was provided by the arrival of Lucy and Robert Ferrars, who lost no time in extending their attentions to their elder brother. Hard upon their settling at the inn, they announced their intent to call at Delaford Parsonage.

Elinor reassured her husband, for she was equal to the effort.

In vain. Mrs. Robert Ferrars' appearance—as ever, she unveiled herself in the smartest of gowns and bonnets, and today especially she carried with her a white satin reticule to proclaim her alertness to London's vogue—in combination with her new authority of voice, her crisp address—in short, her superiority and unmistakable consequentiality— must directly bring tumult to their reunion.

She entered Delaford Parsonage with a flurry and was enraptured, her enthusiasm for it chimed out to her husband in such phrases as, "How very quaint" and "How snug and tidy a house" they saw before them. What else might then be left but for the addition of congratulations upon her sister Elinor's domestic artistry.

"My dear," pronounced she, "I cannot imagine how you do manage it? You are, there is little question, an example to us all, the cleverest young woman among us. But in such restricted circumstances as these, I can only wonder that you keep your equanimity. You are to be commended, and heartily! I should be reduced by the challenge. My own husband, it is true, often declares that small quarters do not diminish *true* comfort. *He* would as lief dwell in a hut as in a palace."

In the silence that followed, she continued, turning to her husband and smiling sweetly, "Dearest Robert, can you picture yourself and your own chosen loved one abiding cozily in peace, so near to happy villagers?"

Robert, who was walking about with his brother, paying little heed to his wife's effusions, heard her not. As for Elinor, she resolutely kept to her purpose. She offered her guests refreshment in the tray of cold meats, jellies, and warm rolls that had just been set out in the sitting room, choosing next to lead her husband's former betrothed out to the back parlor to their vista, to discourse upon the never-ceasing changes in light, the colors of the seasons in the fields and on the hills beyond.

Yet Lucy's animation could not thereby be stayed. She directed her admiration to Edward's library—the many volumes she noted as they had turned about in his study.

"Dear sister," said she, "how charmingly like your learned husband to insist upon so many and such heavy tomes, even in these confined quarters. Having known Edward in his student years, I can remember that the dear fellow could not be detached from his precious books, and alas, nor can he now, it seems."

Her next observation delighted this lady most of all, and she glanced in her husband's direction in search of plaudit for its cleverness. "Now I think upon it," Lucy remarked, "in having chosen the clergy for a life's work, a parson might find one book and one only, to suffice *his* need."

This last cavil tried even Edward's patience, so well did it demonstrate how insincerity allied with ignorance must prosper when it went unchecked.

Robert Ferrars, happily oblivious to his wife's want of grace, chose at this juncture to enlarge upon a subject closer to them both.

"I know you will be pleased to learn, brother, that since I first heard of your determination to join your respected calling—together with your retreat from the responsibility of managing our family's future prospects—I have made great strides in preparing myself for that weighty obligation. I willingly confess to you, brother, how little I considered myself suited either by temperament or talent. Now all that is forgotten.

"My removal to London has no less than promised the Ferrar's prosperity. Why, only strolling through the shrubbery at Vauxhall, or mingling with the lowly sort in other parts of the town, I have studied current developments; in short, I am privy to information of the most useful kind. Lord Sutherland himself, when he sat with me not a fortnight ago to be silhouetted at Mr. Meirs' in the Strand, told me of a most modern machinery now being introduced for the enhancement of the soil. And dining at the Burnsides' last week, I was one of the few privileged to hear of possibilities concerning investment in the best line of racing ponies now bred in England. What good fortune that I presently hold such informed acquaintance! Even Lucy, as she accompanies me often to Almack's, has turned the dance to good account; she listens to intelligence passing between the ladies. How little of such pertinence is to be had here in the country."

Edward was naturally made curious by this speech.

"And how, brother, have you chosen to apply all this news to the security of our father's assets?"

That moment Mrs. Ferrars returned from her morning's excursion with her nephew George, something distracted, her color high. Their greeting exchanged, refreshment taken by the latecomers, Robert, smiling, addressed his mother.

"I have only now been describing to my brother, dear Madam, the good fortune that has come to us since Lucy's and my extended stays in the capital, how watchful supervision has made our Ferrars position ampler than ever before."

She, more aroused than any had ever seen, unfolded a letter and held it aloft. "It has only lately been revealed to me, my fair son and heir, and by your own sweet sister, just how *you* see fit to secure our posterity. If *faro,* or *quinze,* and dicing in London, together with high stakes wagering among the bull-baiters, or the bare-fisted fighters up and down the length of the countryside, are to be the means, then perhaps you are correct. Worse, if this gaming has led to deception, and even *forgery,* as my Fanny hints, then surely you can be named master of your art. But, good Sir, I can not, nor will I allow the honorable name of the Ferrars to be reduced to decadence and disgrace.''

Gathering herself up in fury, she stalked from the room.

Part Three

13

Margaret's boast to her sisters of her new resolve towards greater industry was not after all idle. Only lately had she comprehended that dedication to her studies, and more especially to her drawing, was her one safeguard—in truth, her only fortification—against the tedium of the Barton Park society in which she moved. And when, some days after the ball, her mother reminded her of the urgency of a prompt return there, she found herself not a little distraught.

Having heard from her sister so much made of the distinguished portrait painter now engaged in taking Marianne's likeness, she had hoped to observe something of his technique before her return to Devonshire. But the ball had intervened, and she had not yet been fortunate enough to overlook so much as a single sitting. Glimpsing an opportunity to prolong her stay at Delaford, she made haste to avail herself of it.

"I do so long, Mama, to observe a true artist!"

cried she to that good lady. "Marianne assures me that he is the finest master at the craft, and within the week returns here from his studio in London. I can hardly await the hour when I might study such a man at work. Why, if I am at all fortunate, dearest Mama, he may even deign to glance at one or another of my poor efforts, or, dare I hope for it, offer me instruction. Sweet mother, if you could but spare me from home but a little longer, I promise to apply myself and derive every profit from this good fortune."

How might Mrs. Dashwood refuse her daughter's plea? She would herself make haste towards their house in Devonshire to attend to her workmen in the reconstruction of her stairwell, while Margaret, to her own and sister's delight, might be allowed to linger still at Delaford.

A very grand Sir Thomas Stevenson made his arrival as appointed. A man of considerable importance in his profession, he had already served at court and enjoyed royal patronage, triumphing in the best society with his depictions of figures of nobility and fashion alike. He set directly to work in the back parlor well in time for the light he sought; nor was it his habit, he made it immediately evident, to permit any casual intrusion upon his sessions.

Quickly, therefore, did the grand gentleman indicate his displeasure at the sight of Margaret perched beside *his* subject.

"Mrs. Brandon, this will not do," said he. "I quite assure you that my every experience of portraiture has served to demonstrate that even so much as allowing more than *one* lady in the room at a time only succeeds in bringing on unseemly fits of chit-chat and such foolish asides as vex my patience. Moreover, when such young ladies are related by blood, their fluttery displays become the more insupportable. Your sister, Madam, would do far better to walk out into the brisk air, while we pursue our proper business together.''

Margaret hung her head, crestfallen at these words. The fair Mrs. Brandon, indefatigable as ever, must plead in her sister's favor. ''You do mistake Miss Dashwood's purpose, dear Sir,'' protested she, ''this young lady so admires your artistry that she would dare not so much as speak in your presence, less disturb your art. Indeed, she considers such brilliance as yours to be nothing short of sacred. Do you not, dear Margaret? I believe, Sir, such is her devotion, that she should be content, if only you permit it, merely to sit silently at your feet the day long.''

What ordinary human being—nay, such an exacting eye as this, and himself an architect of beauty—might resist so fair an intermediary? At this sweet appeal, he looked for the first time towards Margaret, and saw that while her sister's might be seen as the fairer countenance—and altogether a complement to his brush and palette—still, the younger lady's own features were far from ill-favored. Moreover, if her sister's words were indeed true, they betokened not only a serious cast of mind, but a judgment in art and its practitioners that was unimpeachable.

"For you alone, Mrs. Brandon," conceded the grudging Sir Thomas, "the young lady may observe," only perforce to add, "and who knows, she may yet be recoverable from the too-common empty-headedness of your sex."

Thus was it that these daily sessions did progress, even with the young visitor in steady attendance. And Sir Thomas was heard to make no more objections, as Margaret faithfully attended his every gesture. As the days passed, his temper was transformed by her regard, so much so that, on occasion, he looked upon her *almost* kindly. He presently took to discoursing to both ladies upon what he meant to reveal by this or that turn of the head or curl of finger; as well as—something more eloquently—"the current poverty of art in their own age"—those wild notions of the new artists, and the appalling lack of discipline he saw among these paltry pretenders.

Margaret remained dutifully, unobtrusively silent, listening to the master's pronouncements, and if she found herself in agreement with little that she *heard* from him, she was yet overwhelmed by what miracles she *saw* in his performance. Intently, she watched while his genius caught every nuance of her sister's expression, her garments, her surroundings. And despite the indignation she felt for his words, her admiration of such mastery grew.

One day, to the astonishment of both sisters, Sir Thomas thrust into Margaret's hand a pen, and set down before her an ink well, commanding her to delineate but one feature true to her sister Marianne. "Here before you," announced he, "is a perfect test of your eye, a face intimate to you in its every particular from your infancy. I have undraped for you my own powers. Now let us see what you comprehend of them."

How he then scoffed at her handiwork! Shaking his head, to conclude solemnly, "Thus you yourself demonstrate, Miss Dashwood, how little one of your sex fathoms profundity in art. To be sure, this ladylike accomplishment, well enough executed. I will own that it is prettily done, and with an energy, indeed, even some resemblance to the subject. Yet, dear lady, look how you have failed to render the set of your sister's cheek, the curve of her lip. Miss Dashwood," he sighed, "here is skill adequate for a common draughtsman—a talent which serves where subtlety is wanting. In short, I fear you do not read a face."

Here he broke off. "But how foolish was I to expect from cherished ladies to understand ardor—to glimpse the artist's soul. After all, how might we doubt, Miss Dashwood, that your own sex knows nothing of resolution, so entirely committed is it to the moment."

Margaret received these arrogant words in great perturbation. While she had felt all the gratitude of instruction from one whose line was subtle, whose eye was superior, and whose hand agile—such gifts as his were a privilege to behold—she had yet not anticipated the harshness as lay beneath the genius.

It made her understand of a sudden that her own first flights towards that intense world he described were those of the fledgling.

Swiftly following upon this emotion came resentment. Well it was for *him,* an acknowledged genius, to bask in his mastery.

"Sir," she ventured, "you yourself may be among those chosen for art by divine hand. For me, the pleasure of sketching lies as much in its doing as in the finished result. I delight in it as blissful release from the sameness of everyday. Ah, good sir, will you so condemn all of us who dabble in your art? Or, is it only those of *my* sex who dare to be ardent in their creative purpose? After all, is it so vile to strive for perfection even when it seems unapproachable? In life, as well as art, such enterprise might at least provide an awareness, a shield from the banalities in society that we seem obliged to endure? I cannot aspire to artistry like your own; still, I must beg you, woman though I am, to leave me undiminished such satisfaction as I may find."

There followed a silence. Even the gentleman was taken aback. As for Marianne, her excitement was too much to be kept to herself. Her sister's steadfastness before the hauteur of the great man brought admiration from an impassioned Mrs. Brandon.

"Margaret," she laughed, as soon as they were alone again, "you do astonish me. I hardly knew you to entertain notions such as these, nor thought you capable of expressing them with eloquence before so formidable an adversary. My once so-biddable, silly little sister, what can have possessed you? Such fearlessness, such determination!''

Margaret's outburst had in truth surprised even herself, and, once uttered, brought tears to her eyes. She must now, for the first time since her visit to her sisters, speak plainly of her own growing perplexities.

''If you wonder at my boldness, Marianne,'' said she, ''it is because you know nothing of my own late experience. You see little of my confinements at Barton Park, or of my despair of escape from them. How should I? Of romance I have little expectation—for long since have I known its treacherous consequence. Yet,'' and she hesitated, ''how should one marry without love... And should love seek me out...I have no money, no connections, no significance.''

''But Sister—'' interjected Marianne, intending comfort.

Yet Margaret persisted, ''And if I delight at your present happiness and that of my sister Elinor's, it is only the more to wonder at the hopelessness of my own situation. I know so little of the world, yet the more I see revealed of it, the less can I see a place for one such as myself. And I seek so very much. For this alone, I have long understood that it is in myself, and myself alone that I shall find safety, or at least solace. And Marianne, surely you will agree,'' catching herself with a smile, ''that after having accommodated myself to Master John Middleton's tantrums, Sir Thomas Stevenson of the Royal Academy is but a jackstraw.''

Her sister now heard this youngest of their family with new attention. From that thoughtless goose so in awe of her sisters had emerged another, someone Marianne recognized hardly at all.

So did these days in Dorset move swiftly forward. Marianne's portraiture progressed, and Margaret continued fascinated by its elegance.

Upon the night of the festivities, it had been fixed that Mrs. Brandon was to call on the Edgertons as soon as she could. Miss Letitia Edgerton had eagerly sought such a visit, and it was not many days after Margaret's contention with the painter that the mistress of Delaford kept her word. She did so in the company of both her sisters.

The day was as yet bright when the three set out towards Atherton Hall, though clouds foretold a menacing afternoon. The sisters were in excellent spirits: Elinor content merely to be away from the irritation lately overtaking her husband's family; Marianne curious to know more of the melancholy Miss Edgerton; and Margaret caught up in the novelty of every encounter in her sisters' company, especially when she recalled her soon-to-be-resumed monotony within the Middleton nursery.

They chattered amiably as their carriage made its way over the several miles of tolerable road, and their gaiety brought their destination swiftly in sight. The house they approached was ample enough of size, though in repair hardly seemed the sort that had, over the years, made any serious demands upon its family's purse. Ramshackle, all but disintegrating, it was a low, dark, structure that presented to its young visitors an aspect of gloom. Nor did closer inspection dispel the impression. High walls enclosed a triangular court, and the few yellow poplars and laurels therein further combined to exclude the daylight. To the sisters, it must appear that the sun had for long been unwelcomed in these quarters.

Fortunate it was, therefore, that before they reached the entry, they could discern the figure of Letitia Edgerton already awaiting them, and her greeting dispersed the initial chill of its setting.

The group was soon joined by the elder Edgertons, tea and biscuits brought, and the ladies cheered the more by the immediate and most hearty reaffirmation by Mr. Edgerton of his delight at once more enjoying the friendship of the new master of Delaford House.

"I am pleased, Mrs. Brandon," began he, "to see the Colonel's recovery of a fine estate, together with the good name of his family. So long was the Brandon property neglected by his brother, and his father before that. Your husband will, I trust, soon be revered as the thoughtful patron of a county well tended."

As quickly as these civilities were accomplished, he must turn to his own sweet preoccupation—for he reveled in his daughter's late achievements in the neighborhood. Such enterprise as she possessed, he assured the sisters, such changes as he had seen effected. Had she not been responsible for the renewed attentions of each neighborhood farmer to his children's growth?

"Veritably, she is their mentor. None manage without her advice. Why, even our apothecary, Mr. Hallett, has frequent recourse to her help. I assure you, ladies, her knowledge and skill have become legendary."

Miss Edgerton at these words crimsoned over. Her father, she protested, was given to exaggeration. True, she *tried* her best, but too often the ignorance of those she served stood sorely in her way. Only that day, she had witnessed, upon rounds with Mr. Hallett, a most distressing case of an infant stricken by the *red gum.*

"The poor child," sighed she, "was all over rash, and so young he knew not how to leave off scratching. I made haste to pare back his little fingernails, and anointed him with the proper liniment, which seemed to bring some comfort. But I fear he will grow up sadly marred. These children, you see, are so little attended by their parents. And there is small wonder to it, as there are so very many of them for their mothers to look to."

Mr. Edgerton now returned his attention to his guests, and bowing to Elinor, said, "Easily may Mrs. Ferrars comprehend my daughter's travails, for of her good services in her own parish, we also hear much. How well we know, alas, that a clergyman's work is never at an end, and, for that matter, nor is his good wife's assistance. But *you,* Mrs. Brandon," turning then to Marianne, "are more privileged in the choice of your pursuits. Letitia has described to us your enthusiasm at the ball when you learned of her benevolent enterprise; might we make bold to enlist you further for help among our farm families?"

Since her splendid marriage and removal to Dorset, Marianne's demeanor had, it has often been observed, softened considerably. Impulsive her temper remained, and her host's words, though innocently spoken, caught her up.

"Why, Sir," said she stirred, "you must not suppose that my own days are so filled with nothing but the idle choosing of colored chintz for a patchwork, or even at endless practice at my instrument. I do assure you I need not venture as far as your needy county: alas, there are yet services aplenty to be discharged daily among our own good villagers at Delaford."

Then, recollecting Miss Edgerton's talk of excursions even farther afield, she altered her tone. "Miss Edgerton did speak to me of one such errand of mercy which especially aroused my compassion," confessed she, "and that, a visit to a friend in sorry circumstances in Brighton. I myself have an interest in this sad lady, and would willingly arrange, no matter the distance, to accompany her there."

Miss Edgerton heard her, but only inclined her head. The conversation turned to other matters.

The charge of reserve has not infrequently been laid to the eldest of the Dashwood sisters, and Elinor *had* heard this exchange with alarm. However, she made no sign to Marianne. It was not until their journey home that she dared comment to her sister upon the subject.

"My dear Marianne, you will forgive my speaking plainly. I do know you to possess the most generous of hearts—to wish to be of service where you feel most deeply. Sister, I cannot but surmise the identity of this sad lady in Brighton, and I must caution you in this. Marianne, are you certain you wish to bring to the fore that from the past which can only prove most painful? And can it be wise to intercede where your good husband himself has not suggested? Miss Edgerton appears to be a woman of sense, one that sees peril in impulse, for plainly she shares my foreboding."

Marianne flushed, and managed no response. Whether she allowed the justice of her sister's reproof was not certain. Still, as the three traveled towards home under a lowering sky, their mood was sober. They rode together in thoughtful silence.

14

Customarily made much of is the consolation of return to home and hearth. Especially after an absence, a warm welcome and secure place within its bosom is ever assured there. For Margaret Dashwood, it was the comfort of familiarity that must sustain her against the spiritlessness she knew to reign. Moreover, her mother's need was entirely in earnest, and even provided for her some unexpected occupation.

In truth, Margaret arrived to find Mrs. Dashwood in a veritable pother. When she had first embarked upon her undertaking to improve their much-loved cottage, she had advertised her eagerness to hear judgments on the matter from her friends. Alas, the lady's character being of that goodness—that openness of mind—to attend readily to all, she quickly discovered herself meditating with equal ardor upon each proposal presented to her, no matter how ambitious or ingenious.

By the time of her daughter's coming, so lost was

she in the contemplation of the many excellent opinions upon what *absolutely* could not be neglected in her restoration effort, that she was driven almost to distraction. But then, as she soon lamented to her much-awaited youngest, she well understood that decisions of such a special nature as these were scarcely of the sort that any lady should properly be asked to make alone.

"Think upon it, my child," began she upon Margaret's arrival, "that a poor widow should so be put to the test. I have seen many trials since the death of your dear father, but this exceeds my every expectation. You cannot know how dearly was I in need of your counsel, Margaret, when contemplating the broadening of the shrubbery walk. Lady Brunton, you see, was entirely urgent in her entreaties. Such an entrance, to be sure, must provide our snug home with the proper stature it has so long lacked. Yet Lady Middleton is adamant that I must address my concentration towards the stairway; and she is after all our proprietor. I could not agree more with both ladies; yet even now, as the work progresses, I wonder whether these improvements might have been the most requisite of our needs."

So was Margaret immediately engulfed upon her return to Barton Park, and, in truth, glad of it. To make herself useful to her mother, through her own steadiness and practicality, and to bring calm to circumstances already well out of hand, was occupation worthy enough for any loving daughter.

"Do you not think, Mama, that we might consider greater moderation in our plans?" suggested she gently, after she had heard repeated, and many times over, the various alternatives for embellishing the cottage's humble structure—of the elaborate scheme for a wider stairway proposed by Lady Middleton—of the more formal new façade for the cottage urged upon her mother by the Comtesse du Plessy—and near a dozen others besides.

"While I most certainly agree with our informed friends that the style of a Repton is most admirable," she continued, "perhaps *we* ourselves, in our more modest edifice, need not aspire to it. And must the stairway, after all, be formed entirely to resemble the Middletons' grand one, or would that be not altogether appropriate, as it ascends but to our cozy rooms? Might we not do better to study our own needs more particularly, since we are only two?"

And so soothing her mother into composure and returning her to some semblance of reason and economy, she was now able to dispatch the workmen into *such* doable compromise as attended to widening the stairway, while at the same time maintaining attention to the Dashwood pocket allowance *and* the rustic look of their simple house.

Far less effectable, despite every good resolution on her part, were Margaret's efforts to resume a companionship with her hearty relative, Sir John Middleton. Too excessive had been the warmth of his welcome—awaiting her at the cottage's door as she descended from the carriage after her journey, interrupting her tender reunion with her mother. All her good intentions sank straightaway.

"Dearest girl," chided he, "if you but knew how

longed for your return has been. You cannot so much as guess at the extent of our solitude. Our evenings have been positively bleak; our days dominated by children's willfulness. With you back among us there is some hope to find once more, the most eligible, gayest young people of the country. The very thought of their liveliness—so lacking in these weeks—gives me spirit. You alone can restore us to the good humor we have been wanting."

Margaret sought a complaisant reply. "Surely you flatter me, good Sir," said she smiling, "since I know well that your own diversions hereabouts are many. Why, I do not doubt that your every waking moment during my absence rang with the sound of the horn. And you, with your children so attentive and ever at your feet—for shame! No, Sir John, I cannot think how your affairs can have altered for as much as an hour while I remained among my sisters at Delaford."

"Well, my child," ran on the good gentleman undaunted, "You will surely concede that we were cruelly abandoned. Our own Lady Clara, for one, has left us, and been gone these weeks, and so too has that diverting young man, the son of our dear Comtesse. He must of course to his duty, a return to his regiment in Brighton. Still, since his departure weeks ago we have heard but twice from this officer, and his mother is near frantic with the worry of it. I assure you, Miss Dashwood, we have suffered. Why, our company is shrunken so one must not of an evening even hope for a table of whist, especially since Mrs. Jennings fails us so often in her fatigue. I can tell you, Margaret, should you not have returned to us, I myself might have given up the struggle and chosen to sleep the winter away like the bear in his cave.''

For Lady Middleton's part, she had much to add to her husband's words, although her own tale was considerably brighter.

"You will, I assure you, Miss Dashwood," began she with pride when next they met, "be much edified by the alterations in the school room since you left. Indeed, I venture to predict you will hardly recognize your former favorites, so much improved have they become under the tutelage of none other than the Comtesse du Plessy herself. That lady has taken them under her wing, aiming to introduce them to the true meaning of cultivation, and this, as only the French understand such matters. The result is blessed harmony. Yes, Miss Dashwood, you will find my darlings charmingly emerged—I confess that so thoroughly has the Comtesse brought them out that at times I hardly know them for mine own.''

And indeed, upon Margaret's arrival the next afternoon in the nursery, she was astonished to find that Lady Middleton had spoken no less than the truth. The children were transformed, and this thanks entirely to the efforts of the redoubtable Comtesse, who, upon first encountering the Middleton children, had been aghast at their forward behavior, and expressed herself to that effect.

"Could the unruliness I observe in this household be the result of that leniency one hears to be so current in the rearing of English children these days?'' she had demanded. ''I warrant you that had they been schooled in the French manner, we should never be witness to such deafening displays of temper. No, if seen at all, our offspring most certainly are not heard from until bidden. Madam, depend upon it, among your better families, you should not encounter such chaos as is encouraged among these, your young people.''

Mrs. Jennings and Lady Middleton, while chagrined at the harshness of this pronouncement, were neither of them entirely surprised by it, or unreceptive to possible remedy. When the Comtesse assured them that she herself was ready to take up the children to reorder their ways—in short, to make them comprehend French manners in their grander aspects before she departed Barton altogether—they were eager to cooperate with her in a stern and rigorous regimen.

So it was that Margaret, upon greeting the heretofore boisterous children, found herself barely acknowledged by them. The two boys bowed from the waist, Mary curtseying prettily, while all murmured together, as if under a spell, a dutiful, almost inaudible, ''Mamzelle?'' Then, upon Margaret's warmly taking Annamaria by the hand, the child stood mute before her as if newly presented, or as one that remembered her not at all. The very formality of the four children made Margaret laugh aloud. In truth, all the while that Comtesse du Plessy was in attendance upon them, John, Annamaria, William, and Mary were perfection itself.

The children were next charged with showing their newest acquisitions. John must list for the adults the names of each of the provinces of France and their best vineyards, while his sister, having put to memory one of La Fontaine's fables, was called upon to recite from The Old Man and the Ass. Both obliged their listeners, after which a beguiled *maitresse* must remind her eager charges how remarkably canny was "the character of the French donkey," before turning her attention once again to the display of their prowess.

There seemed no end to their quizzing by the lady, and to the biddable performance of these hitherto ungovernable children. So much so, that to show her pleasure in their swift advancement—and to delight their mother and grandmother, the Comtesse thought to reward her pupils with an invitation to join the party when tea was finally brought.

Even more notable was their demeanor then. Heard only, in Continental accents, were the children's subdued "s'il vous plait, Madame," their "mercis," and their "enchantés," and when young John in passing the meat pie to the Comtesse mincingly referred to it as "paté," there was nothing but admiration for what seemed a glorious pedagogical feat.

The Comtesse exulted at these effects of her instruction. "So you can see," concluded she, "what good fortune to have the advantages of a Classical education—to have committed to memory every kind of knowledge. That, I must assure you, is the meaning of true learning."

Mrs. Jennings' admiration know no bounds. "Have I not told you how clever is my dear friend? Little that she sets her mind to does not succeed. Never shall I forget how she trained my beloved pug, Sarah. You will not remember my pet," she added, addressing her daughter, "how before the Comtesse undertook her, she simply would not heed."

But the knowledgeable lady had merely begun the young Middletons' reduction. Encouraged, she tenaciously pursued her intention to cultivate their comportment in society at large.

"You will soon understand, young man," she said, addressing the eldest, "that whatever infraction against order and manners occurs among your associates, it will be entirely *your* responsibility, and yours alone. Such is the commission of a family's eldest. We on the Continent understand such matters. In this way it is ascertained that your good parents never need more find themselves troubled by unruly children. Should younger children do themselves harm, it can only be ascribed to the negligence of the eldest. You, John, senior to your brother and sisters, must now take authority, keep the discipline, *never* allow any of your youngers to stray from what you deem proper. You, John Middleton, are the proper guardian of good order."

Given such a mandate, the twelve-year-old needed nothing further. From that moment, he took the children instantly from the company and arraigned them to do his will.

One day, soon after Margaret's return, when she

and her mother had been summoned once more to the Middletons' for tea, Walters burst into the drawing room distraught.

"Madam," said the nurse, out of breath, "I trust you will forgive this intrusion. I have just discovered that young William is locked in the cellar, while his sisters are nowhere to be found, and John refuses me the key!"

Her discomposure moved even Lady Middleton to alarm. Confronted, the boy explained, "I acted quickly and properly. I did my duty, Mama, only to prevent my brother's doing himself an injury jumping from the garden wall. I warned him to come down, but he would continue. I thought best to teach him a lesson. He must cool his heels and so comprehend his folly—disobedience to his brother."

As for Annamaria and Mary, they had escaped from the continual bullying of the boy by hiding in the closet of their room. Poor Walters had given them up after searching an hour together. The newest regime with the eldest son in charge had so exhausted that good woman that she was spent.

When Sir John returned with "the best news ever" for our Margaret—"the imminent arrival of his Lincolnshire friend—a not entirely ill-favored bachelor, of means"—it was with relief that she must gratefully decline his invitation to dine at Barton Hall at week's end.

The reprieve had come that morning in the form of a most welcome letter from Lady Clara Ashburton. It had read,

Dear Miss Dashwood, I have been these weeks in London and can happily report that I am now finally able to remove from its hustle for a sojourn beside the sea. I had regretted that our happy acquaintance was cut short by your own departure. I trust that you might prevail upon your mother to permit you to join me in a visit to Brighton. There, we two together may continue to stroll at leisure, take the sea air, and best of all, resume our talks to our heart's content. Do arrange to come, for I dearly seek your company.

Your friend, etc.

15

It was not a fortnight afterward that Lady Clara Ashburton had installed herself comfortably into rooms in Gardiner Street at Brighton. Her quarters pleased her, being, she considered, set suitably apart from the crush of that watering-place's most noble and fashionable society, while just close enough to the Steine for her daily promenade. Despite every chill in the November air, that hearty lady would venture forth into its salty briskness, willing to brave any weather for a whiff of the sea. Even one morning, under the watchful management of her landlord and the attendants he brought forward for the purpose, she enjoyed being dipped into the salt water itself, and found herself the more invigorated for the experience.

By the time her young friend Margaret Dash-wood made her own arrival some days later, Lady Clara could boast that she had given herself over to all the enjoyment of air and exercise. She was impatient to introduce that young lady to their whole-some merits.

"I caution you, Margaret," began she, "that I am become something of an apostle of Brighton. Nature has marked it out—bestowed upon it the finest, purest breeze on the coast—and all at a bare sixty miles from London! I see you wearied by your journey, and dispatch you instantly to your rest, that you may enjoy the greater vigor tomorrow. I must warn you, my dear, that we start early."

Grateful for the warmth of her friend's greeting and diverted by the fervor of her tone, Margaret retired content, to appear fresh on the morrow.

Their converse at breakfast was easy. Lady Clara, in high spirits, was eager to hear the news from Barton. She laughed most heartily at Margaret's de-scription of the alteration in the young Middletons.

"But if any were capable of effecting such a turnabout," concluded she, "it might well be my formidable friend Isabel. Too well I know that some might consider grounds for ridicule her proud man-ner—her French airs—her fashionable person. In-deed, I confess, there are times when I find them so myself. But do not take her, Margaret, for a woman of less mettle than is there. My friend has seen much, suffered much—and has come forth with honor. Beneath all the pose is a person of un-exceptionable substance. As," with a glance at her young visitor, "beneath his own easy charm is her son Mr. du Plessy."

Margaret colored at her reference and looked away in some confusion. Had the lady observed her contrary, ill-sorted feelings towards this young man?

Happy therefore was she when Lady Clara rose to lead her out to the sights of the resort. As they donned their warmest attire and tied their shawls and bonnets against the wind, Margaret was exultant, for the first time in some years truly at one with a companion.

So did they set out to their affairs in the brilliant light of the sea. Emerging from Gardiner Street onto the Steine, the young woman gazed in wonder, as at an apparition, for gleaming before them rose the onion domes of the Prince's stables, and an extravaganza of pagodas that with the Marine Pavilion was his house. She had heard tell of these marvels—the continual improvements of the many architects engaging their flights of fancy, all the more encouraged by their sovereign—but to stand in the presence of this private kingdom was awesome.

"A fine vision from here, and, I am told, there is all the celestial harmony of the Orient within," said Lady Clara. But as they walked on, the lady grew thoughtful. "Yes, there is, and I trust always will be, the salubrious call of the sea, to which, happily, even our dear Regent must succumb. Yet I fear, a less remarked upon phenomenon is effected by the sea air. It unbridles every discipline. In these days, I warrant you, you shall see loosed here the most flamboyant of behaviors, even as in London itself. Unlike our more gentle towns, Brighton's liveliness encompasses entertainment for the tastes of a variety of gentlemen and ladies. There are many among them who frequent the racing at the Downs, the card playing or gaming clubs, or entertainment at concerts and the theater, and who, for their part, will never so much as once come forward to breathe this bracing air or take the medicinal baths.''

Still, to Margaret, every sight she looked upon seemed fantastic, the lavish shops they passed, the many fashionable strollers in the narrow lanes, and even the numbers of young men in their red coats, plumed hats, and Hessian boots, who saluted them as they passed. Lady Clara had determined that for their first outing, they should proceed only so far as the new library, where she might have the opportunity to recover herself after such exertion, while she sat comfortably perusing the latest newspapers from London.

It was here too that the good lady proposed—as was her duty to her friend—to consult the book of the Master of Ceremonies, and thus learn of the arrivals in Brighton, as well as the events to be anticipated within the Assembly Rooms.

''Margaret, you shall find gathered within it the most sociable groups,'' she explained. ''These rooms are of appeal to our more genteel society, for the library is Brighton's own particular retreat, a place to see and be seen. You might even notice,'' she added half-smiling, ''that within its precincts far less attention is given to reading matter than to chattering *sotto voce,* a hum that is all about, never ceasing.''

Indeed, by the time the ladies had collected them-

selves for their return to their lodgings, they were
privy to a deal of intelligence, not least of which
was the imminent arrival of the Prince, together
with his assemblage of retainers. They heard too of
a performance of *The Double Elopement,* not to be
missed, at the Theatre Royal in New Road, and had
even ascertained from Captain Wade, the gentleman
in attendance there, that the Assembly Rooms were
by week's end to be the scene of a grand gala.

"Your protégée," said he, glancing at Margaret
after she had been presented, "must find our company acceptable, for all your best families from the
shires, are ever secured among us in Brighton.
There can be no better place for a young lady to
encounter them than at our evenings at the Assembly Rooms."

With considerable merriment did Margaret hear
him term "protégée," and as to the acceptability of
association with the shires' "best families," she
could hardly see an objection.

Only shortly thereafter, upon contentedly leaving
this establishment, did the ladies come upon yet
another group of red-coated officers just then approaching. The impression that they gave was, however, less than pleasing. An unruly collection, their
converse in the corridor was loud, even boisterous,
and there was an unseemly informality in their
exchange.

Lady Clara, in her anxiety to conduct her young
friend with dispatch past the soldiers, let fall her
scarf. Suddenly there was a gallant rush as these
officers came to her aid. How politely did they

scurry and, bowing to the lady, present her with it again.

For that brief moment, Lady Clara remained with the gentlemen that she might thank them for their courtesy. And only then did Margaret recognize among them a strikingly tall officer whose face was entirely familiar to her. There before her stood the smartly uniformed William du Plessy himself.

Separating himself from his companions, he darted across the entry and greeted them.

"Can this be?" he laughed, "Or like the rest of this phantasmagoric Brighton, is it a mere illusion of pleasure?" There he appeared, as ever at ease, addressing himself to Lady Clara, yet fixing his gaze only on Margaret. "Am I truly blessed by such a fortunate meeting?"

Mr. du Plessy's manly beauty, Margaret had early determined to resist; but so unsettling was his chance appearance here that she need avert her face. His high color, his proud bearing, that familiar frankness of approach revealing his delight in the encounter could overtake any retreat. It was devastating.

How difficult she found it to manage even a word. Composing herself, she assured him of his mother's presence at Barton, and that she had lately seen her in good health.

Lady Clara's easy cordiality intervened to rescue Margaret, and the officer proceeded at his most engaging.

"Our leisurely walks together in the Devonshire country have been warmly in my recollections these weeks," said he. "And here before me are the very companions with whom I enjoyed them. What good fortune that without further delay we might now resume our wanderings together, dear ladies. To that end, may I presume to call upon you tomorrow morning early, to offer my services in exploring this wild coast? I am, you must be certain, at your disposal in every moment I am spared from the duties of my regiment."

Margaret welcomed his confident suggestion with an eagerness that surprised even herself. Brighton, it would seem, had already worked such a happy change that she felt herself almost carefree.

As for Lady Clara, she expressed her delight at the prospect by fixing the next day for the young gentleman at their lodging in Gardiner Street.

16

The renewed appeal for Margaret Dashwood of William du Plessy had at least withstood suspicion and scrutiny during the next several hours. And when he arrived promptly the following day to call upon the ladies, his demeanor manifested itself as unexceptionable still. So agreeably did he talk of their time in Dorset, so jocularly of Sir John's hospitality, so deferentially of his mother's unceasing privations, so whimsically of the comforts of home—and withal—of the alternative delights in frequently venturing *from it* in travel—that Margaret found herself better entertained than she had supposed possible.

There was, in fact, no subject that seemed unbroachable for this fortuitously reunited party of acquaintances. Lady Clara watched her young friend's engagement in their exchange with some surprise, since she remembered a less trusting participant in such intercourse whilst they were together in Dorset. The wise lady had earlier marveled at Margaret's seeming determination to dismiss this young man's every approach as dalliance. Yet observing the pair today, she saw a Miss Dashwood unquestionably dazzled by the officer's sophistication, his wit, above all his decidedly candid responses to inquiry.

How he did delight them with his incisive depiction of the best of Brighton's seasonal society, making sport of the comings and goings of the elegant families presenting themselves with regularity from London or from the North.

"You might not credit it, ladies, but in this far corner of England there is no lack of tumult. Each day that dawns—and no matter the pretext—whether it be to welcome the Bessboroughs' party or the Ponsonbys just arrived, you will find the Assembly Rooms ever in a blaze of scarlet, abuzz with the latest dispute over which of the young ladies present has read the best novel of the season, or even that *she* who shall fall desperately in love by evening's end. Above all, one must always consider—never forget—just how urgently each attendant provides for her diary's pages at midnight."

Clearly encouraged by the effect of his raillery, he went on, even to hint—if with a delicacy intended to spare their modesty—at those *other* much advertised diversions of the resort so generously provided his military comrades.

"We of the army do have our share in its temptations. I confess to it." At this did he halt to add discreetly, "And you may well imagine the various difficulties created by *their* easy availability."

All curiosity, Lady Clara would certainly wish to know more. "Do your fellow officers, then," she asked, "frequent the very clubs of which our Prince is, I am told, himself most fond? And has His Royal Highness too been present at your gaming?"

"For myself, I cannot boast of such an encounter," responded he, "though I must own that my visits to these establishments have been common enough. Yet, in truth, it is not so much for the sport itself that I attend as in hope of finding tolerable cuisine. For it is only at the Regent's clubs, Madam, I can assure you, that we of the Dragoons are fortunate to gain such relief from the sparse and monotonous daily rations to be had within the encampment."

His grimace brought sympathy from them both, and elicited the promise of better remedy in the form of an invitation to dine with those ladies themselves. Yet the elder of the two, her interest whetted, must even now press her pursuit. Had the officer himself been privileged to penetrate the much-talked of halls of the Prince's private seaside palace? "We hear such tales of brilliantly colored lanterns, of dragons, and banquets fit for an Oriental potentate."

"Ever since our Major General's glorious victories in Spain," he replied, "I have had the good fortune to accompany him as he waits upon our Regent at his retreat. I was at first, I do confess it, unprepared for such grandeur as was to be seen there. You, dear ladies, may already have enjoyed the sight of the stables. To look upon *those stables* from the outside it would appear that the Prince's horses are better housed than himself. Still, could you have witnessed the scene *within*, as I have done, and it including so many of my former countrymen—émigrés as they are—what a different picture would emerge for you.

"Truly, it has often seemed to us mere soldiers that we enter there another world. So much bamboo and tea wood—and those odd, Oriental pier tables. The *treillage*, the *fretwork*, such enrichments as I know not even the names of! Why," continued he mischievously, "in one audience with my own Major General Wellesley, our Prince sat in company with a newly rescued nobleman, the Comte de Lisle. Yet these great gentlemen were robed in shining *Mandarin* court dress, amidst a splendor of sabers and swords embossed with gold." Here he broke off, looking to enjoy the effects of this tale upon his admirers.

"What a curious sight! More remarkable even," laughed the officer, "was how not so much as *mention* of this circumstance was made by any there, and certainly not by my plain-spoken commander, for whom that day was, as ever, duty and no more. For myself, I warrant you, I thought it was a most peculiar state to be found in for *any* Frenchman, nay even any Englishman, for that matter."

Lady Clara, much diverted by this vision of exotic entertainment, could only exclaim upon the sometimes singularly odd properties of Brighton's air. She added playfully, "But then, perhaps your former countrymen might simply have fared better had they taken refuge in London, while their champion—as I understand His Royal Highness to be—was in residence at Carlton House. There, I am told, our European decor and manner yet prevail."

The amiable lady would herself acquaint him with another fantastical Brighton, one *she* knew. There were, she explained, those daily wonders to be witnessed in her own restorations—the infallibility of dips into the waves, not to speak of the tastings of sea water. Had he some familiarity with the enormous power of that beverage to treat every bilious rheum?

"Yes, Mr. du Plessy, we do so fancy our remedial seaside shores. I do not wonder at a Frenchman's presence, although for the exiles," and here the lady turned serious, "if you come to it, alas, their presence with us is accounted for less by a search for pleasure than by flight from the miseries and misfortunes of war."

By this the officer was sobered, and seemed for a moment unaware of his company altogether; but the lady's mood continuing gay, he rallied.

"Indeed, Sir," persisted she, "Brighton blissfully releases among us those playful natures that must remain elsewhere hidden. We can only cheer those who demand the purples and scarlets—caprices of every sort. When you do contemplate it, perhaps this is the truest mark of nobility. Our sovereign-apparent, it would seem, is of just such an artistic temperament, and you will know surely that such is ever unpredictable. Why, the good Prince's imagination enlivens us all, and turns windy Brighton into Walpole's wondrous kingdom of *Serendip* itself!''

Her companions applauded her sanguine reflections. Moreover, Lady Clara's enthusiasm reminded Mr. du Plessy of the interest of his young friend. Addressing himself to the artistic bent of that mercurial young person before him, he turned their converse. ''And do you still, Miss Dashwood, even in this season's changeable weather, regularly walk out with your sketch book as you did when last we met?'' he said, looking full at her.

''More than ever, sir,'' responded she, pleased by his recollection. But recalling the dire pronouncement by a master at Delaford—continued somewhat subdued, ''Why only lately was I privy to the counsel of the great painter Sir Thomas Stevenson, whilst he labored at a portrait of my sister at Delaford House.''

''How delightful must that have been for you, Miss Dashwood, and what inspiration might it not provide you in your work.''

''Ah, to the contrary, dear sir. I was early reprimanded by Sir Thomas as one superficial, devoid of judgment; in short, a woman and amateur. The great man boasts that ladies are frivolous by nature, thus in no way capable except at their needlework,'' she pointed to the sampler in her hands. ''My work he *would* see; yet when I produced it, it was scanted. How I was lectured upon divinity in the True Life of Art! And now, Mr. du Plessy, I dare only present myself to you a mere appreciator— never, never again creator. In fact, I must hereby dedicate myself to perfecting my skill with the needle alone, lest I be seen as aberration in the eyes of such a Master, and, I surmise, the world at large.''

He smiled at her mocking tone, but was unwilling to be amused. ''With all due respect to the eminence of the artist, I must observe that had this gentleman the slightest acquaintance with the Continent, where the brilliance of our ladies has for generations drawn the attention of the civilized world, his arrogance might have been checked.''

Margaret observed his ardor in her cause as he spoke with feeling.

''As I am bred an Englishman—nor is it said with regret that I myself cannot pretend to their great sophistication—my admiration for such subtlety of thought and manners as is theirs will ever intrude. In France, at least, for generations past, few such distinctions have been made regarding the talent of their cultivated ladies. It is, in truth, to the many faculties of your own sex we look for philosophic wisdom, for yours is an understanding of the art of living profounder than we ourselves may claim.

''No, Miss Dashwood, I should conclude that any spirited young person might well have trimmed the sail of that Royal Academician of yours. If only he had been reminded of his fellow artist Reynolds' understanding that, 'art in its perfection is not ostentatious; it lies hid, and works its effect, itself unseen.' Genius or no, how might we not wonder at a man who pronounces so against womankind?''

His hostess and her young friend heard him

something astonished. Before long the friends came to talk of his wish to serve them in their wanderings beside the sea. And were the ladies fond of the theater? He was, of course, unsure how long he might be privileged to do so, since his command was fixed and many depended upon him; yet while they were in the vicinity, he could wish only for such good fortune as to attend them.

Her elation at his words so startled her that Margaret remained silent and kept firmly at her needlework. Here was intelligence coupled with wit, even a notable good sense. She felt more contentment with the sudden change in her lot than prudence allowed. Despite every caution, she found herself inclined.

Part Four

17

Margaret's communications from her mother during her sojourn in Brighton continued both frequent and reassuring. Not only were the modified improvements on Barton Cottage progressing apace, but even more miraculously, Mrs. Dashwood now found no daily necessity to alter her decisions regarding their scope. So ran the latest,

> *Lovely child, you need have no care of it, as I am confidently in command over Master Frost's artistry. Instead, you must determine to profit yourself from the uplifting company of Lady Clara, and yet the while permit yourself exposure to all the constitutional potential of the seaside.*
>
> *Ah, how often have I heard extolled the great benefits there to be had! Take, for example, fish-roe or fish liver—never you mind their taste—they can make the teeth sparkle. And to be sure, my sweet daughter, not of the*

*very least, is that while so in attendance, you
may partake as fortification of the miraculous
waters. Such frail creatures are we, after all,
who knows when we may succumb to the me-
grim and the cold humors. So my love, such a
security against them is ever urgent.*

Oh, gratifying circumstance! Not since the loss
of her dear father could Margaret remember such
lightheartedness as she now felt. Can it be wondered if it began to seem to our heroine that her life
had taken another direction, her luck a remarkable
turn. To be in the steady company of one such as
Lady Clara Ashburton here in the bracing wind that
blew in from the sea was pleasure enough, far better
than she could have imagined even a few short
weeks ago. But there were too the sweetly unsettling civilities—nay, attentions—as Mr. du Plessy
proffered. These brought an intoxication visible in
her stride, her speech, her letters to her family—her
each undertaking. Even more notable was the radiance of her look.

In the morning Margaret awoke in high spirits,
ever in readiness for excursion, exercise, or any ad-
venture her friend might invent. And Lady Clara
willingly obliged with designs for many such entertainments, from strolls upon the nearby Steine for
a view of the fisher folk at their nets, to expeditions
by carriage to ferret out exquisite remedies at the
nearby spa of Hove, and from thence to elegant
evenings at the local theater, or to sparkling balls
in the Assembly Rooms.

Her pleasure made our young lady expansive. She allowed herself to fret less and enjoy more. The care of so perceptive an advisor as her hostess eased all former constraint.

As to the Lady, she too felt comfortably attended. It had occurred to her that in Margaret, she might have stumbled upon the very child she herself would have reared had she been fortunate in life and had she a daughter of her own.

"Yet," she herself marveled aloud one morning, "I can not but wonder at discovering you so, and there in Devonshire amongst my quaint schoolmates! How unlikely a setting to have afforded such a lively companion of my age. You do comprehend my very thoughts as though we had been familiars of a lifetime."

The lady's fondness, and more particularly her confidence in Margaret's specialty now made deliverance seem complete. It gave to someone whose short history had served only to confuse her a new clarity, and even courage to persevere. For the first time in her life, the youngest Miss Dashwood ventured to trust her own judgment.

To further her delight, there were also cheery letters from "the formidables," as she dubbed her older sisters. Those engaged, laughing epistles could not but divert, even when both of those ladies found themselves submerged in domestic squabble. Elinor wrote of persistent demands made by Edward's mother, the lady's moods, her martial rule. Yet the younger Mrs. Ferrars hardly seemed disgruntled, and certainly never despairing. Forbearance had ever been Elinor's strength in crisis; now, even as her husband, a man of the cloth, preached charity, so could his wife put it to practice. Wrote she,

> As soon as poor Mrs. Ferrars has resolved all those troublesome anxieties regarding her new choice of heir, she will grab up her favorite—with every blessing from us—and be soon away. Once, long ago, the same lady pronounced her elder son "dead" to herself and his family; now, having graciously restored him to life, she can be solaced, certain that he bears her no grudge. This, when reconciliation with him especially assures her he asks little more than that of her.
>
> Of course, you will remember, Margaret, her deferential nephew, Mr. George Osborne, a generally promising and upright young man?—that is, if one overlooks his doggedness in this cause. He dotes upon her, is devoted to her every whim, but since he must hie to his affairs in London—she certain to follow him—we shall once again be left to ourselves in the peaceful countryside to greet winter cozily.

It was not many days after that another missive arrived, this one from a jaunty Marianne.

"How gay has our little one become at her Brighton retreat," she began, and promptly fell to hinting at a happy development of her own, "a little something'' that she wished not as yet to reveal, but would surely be "evident" when next they met.

What Mrs. Brandon *could,* however, agreeably vaunt was the success of their recent celebration in restoring consonance among "les artistes."

"You will by now—can you doubt it?" she said, "have had reports—for they are widespread through the region, that the parish of Parson Ferrars is once more the possessor of 'the most affecting church musicians in all of Devonshire.' For now at least, harmony prevails over dissonance."

Her lively comment she next turned to her young sister's own recent contribution to the skirmishing at Delaford House.

Have you even contemplated your effect upon our great genius? Dear sister, I shudder to think what you might make of Sir Thomas now! His manner is as brusque as before, you understand, but as for his tirade… Ah, Margaret, too long has that good master sought in vain for the sublime. Alas, the task of dealing with the "empty-headedness" of our sex grows burdensome. Angelic his artistry may be, but given such disdain for the half of creation, his soul is doomed to languish here on earth, far from the spheres. Still, the portrait, dear Margaret, the portrait! It will fairly dance down that long gallery wall among the solemn faces of the Brandons. That is, once we have mounted it.

But Margaret, I must now to a serious sub-

*ject. I confess that ever since our visit together
with Miss Edgerton and her family, I have
thought much upon Elinor's advice, even taken
to heart her cautions concerning my wish to
know more of certain unfortunates in Brighton.
Well enough though it be for Miss Edgerton to
persist in excellent ministration to her childhood friend's daughter; for myself, despite
every anxiety of my own regarding the fate of
this lady and her child, I must for propriety's
sake beg to be excused.*

*Yet, Sister, I have the while secured the ex-
act whereabouts of that luckless pair, for loyalty does move me still—and forcefully. Dearest Margaret, I entreat, could you, would you
while there at the shore carry out an errand
in my stead?*

*Such reassurances as you take to the un-
happy lady might perhaps be just the kindness
that I can manage, while maintaining that distance Elinor deems necessary. Since that day,
I am not able to put from my mind her plight.
I do heartily wish the lady well, and would
have her hear of it, just as I am determined,
Margaret, that I must know the whole upon
this sad subject, once and forever.*

> *Your affectionate sister, etc.*

All the pain and distress of her sister's first love
and its betrayal came rushing directly back to Margaret's recollection. Tenderhearted, ever passionate
Marianne. How endlessly had she, a worshipping

child, been instructed by her sister upon the value
of such loyalty, such devotion! Once bestowed, it
must never be abandoned—nor forgotten.

Immediately, therefore, did Margaret resolve to
undertake for her this errand, to bring to these
friends her affectionate greetings, to do everything
in her power to ameliorate the suffering of Eliza
Williams and her child. No one else but Marianne
(though excepting, by necessity, Lady Clara) should
be privy to the knowledge that such an encounter
had occurred. She would see to that.

Before the afternoon was out, she had placed all
before the lady, who apprehended Marianne's concern.

"Indeed, child, you must serve Mrs. Brandon in
this reconciliation. Her delicacy is commendable.
She thinks more of her husband's happiness than
her own."

So did she set forth one morning while her friend
was preoccupied with her medicinal application, to
the address in Preston Road which Marianne had
provided. It was a long walk, and she pursued her
way against the wind. The sharp air brought the
color to her cheeks. Her bonnet sheltered her from
the wet blow as she progressed steadily well beyond the places she had found so stylish and fashionable, towards a grim square where lived the lady.
The house itself stood behind the street; its aspect
was but narrow and mean. Yet there was a respectability about it, a clean entry and scrubbed stair.

She climbed to its top as she had been bidden by
her sister's direction, and knocked. When the door

opened, a kindly, youngish person greeted her, who was neatly if plainly attired in the fashion of a gentlewoman. At her side, holding firmly to her skirts, was a child with great, curious eyes that stared up at their visitor. This lady's surprise at receiving a caller, a perfect stranger, was evident by her startled expression.

Margaret quickly explained her errand. She had only intended to leave her note and some sweets, to return at a more appropriate moment.

Her hostess welcomed her with warmth and invited her into her lodgings, while apologizing for its modest appearance. Indeed, the sitting room she led her to was so small, it was more akin to an entry passage than a place in which to greet a guest. Withal it was comfortably appointed.

"How delightful of Miss Edgerton to send you to us," said Mrs. Williams. "She is by far John's favorite of all our friends, is she not, child?" She thanked her guest for the box of cakes she had brought and promptly offered them.

Though the boy was shy and clung to his mother's knee, he accepted with delight and bowed politely, acknowledging his gratitude. He made no sound, but studied Margaret with intensity. He was some five years of age, altogether fair of color, and his shining blue eyes announced intelligence. There was a familiarity to their look. Margaret could not doubt that striking image which despite the years still inspired such recognition.

Could silence persist while such a child graced the room? It was no time before the ladies were

exchanging pleasantries, and Mrs. Williams, for so
was she referred to, cheerfully set about to make
her visitor easy.

Then Margaret acknowledged their closer ties.
As sister to Mrs. Brandon, the wife of Colonel
Brandon of Delaford in Dorset, she had been
charged to bring to Mrs. Williams her special re-
gards, her fond wishes. And while in the district,
Miss Dashwood assured her, she herself was all eagerness to be of service. She could do no less.

To Mrs. Williams came a look of apprehension;
this, followed by one of pleasure.

"Indeed, the Colonel has been my benefactor
from my youngest days. It is to him that I owe
everything, and because of him that I now persevere. As *he* continues ever our loving mentor, we
want for naught. You see, Miss Dashwood, his feelings for my dear mother and his loyalty towards
myself sustain me. They allow me hope."

Mrs. Williams had indeed learned of the Colonel's marriage, but knew little more. Even, it did
seem, she now confessed with a laugh, that they
saw rather less of him on account of it. "Still," she
added, "it was all to the good, for his lady wife
seems to have effected so sterling a recovery upon
my once forlorn patron that I can only marvel at it.
For one mired in so dark a past as his own, he is
become a happy gentleman. That he laments no
more is for me as heartening as it is admirable. I
know the more delight in salutations from his wife,
your good sister.

"But," bestirring herself, "such a long way have

you come, Miss Dashwood,'' she said, ''if you did
cross the lanes and the windy Crescent in *this* cold.
You will accept a hot beverage and some meats.''

Margaret could not in good grace deny her.

The meanwhile, young John Williams contentedly busied himself with the few playthings he had
brought forth. Margaret wondered at the sufficiency
with which he entertained himself; she had seen
little such industry on the part of the favored children of her acquaintance—in Harry Dashwood or
any of the four Middletons. The place could in no
way serve as nursery. There was little to suit a child
here. Still, he worked at his spillikins, cheerily turning to his blocks when he tired of that employment.

Barely had his mother left the room, when he
rose to the occasion: indeed with some ceremony
he did act the proper host, looking up to Margaret
with his wide eyes, and thanking her for the cakes
she had carried.

''I do so dearly love such a confection,'' said he.
''You left my good Uncle Brandon well, I hope.
How I do await his coming always, for he takes us
to ride about in a barouche. It is a lovely time we
have all together with Mama, when we can see
more of our Brighton.''

Such an attentive manner, such direct speech.
She was taken by the sweetness of his nature.
Surely this child had been plucked from an earlier
time, as from a painting in a cathedral—an angel
alighted, so innocent seemed his gaze. As his
mother returned with a tray, so he resumed his
game, never intruding into their colloquy.

"What contentment there seems in your boy," began Margaret. "Is his nature always so easy?"

"Young John will talk the day long; he is a most agreeable companion. Such is his temperament that it hardly requires commanding. The lad is also blessed with true curiosity; an eagerness to master what he can, such is his relish for every living thing. He is the very sun of my life, and I bask in its light."

Margaret silently admired them: to have so little, yet make so much of what there was!

Mrs. Williams wondered at the occasion of Miss Dashwood's own visit in Brighton in this late season. Might the young lady keep on at the seaside?

"For myself, dear Madam," replied she, "I should remain here as long as I might; but it is not for me to decide. I am at the disposition of a truly remarkable friend, and it is my happy chance to have been reprieved from the doldrums of the country to the excitement of your shore. Here is such constant succession of event: someone appears, someone departs; meeting unpredicted, discoveries made. When one considers the confinement of our Devonshire communities…"

"Indeed, a spa can most certainly boast of every diversion. In this you are precise," mused Mrs. Williams. This brought the lady to a reminiscence of her own gay youth, and that not long ago, for she was even yet not five-and-twenty. She too had then been carried along by friends into revels like these. How well she recollected the delights of her own arrival in the city of Bath.

"I too, Miss Dashwood, was brought out from the country by good friends, and they eager to see me amused and entertained. Alas, for the very young, such excitements come with fancies and folly. If you have ever read *The Beggar Girl* or *Delphine*, or any work of that description, you will recall—at least in these histories—that the heroine never fails to enchant everyone of rank wherever she goes; that enthusiastic companions start up at every step; and that, in short, she is indebted to her lovely face for every good office. Yes, for innocents, for castle builders who imagine life as they read of it in novels, pitfalls are strewn everywhere. Such was my inexperience, that I believed all that I saw and heard.

"But then, Miss Dashwood, *you* need fear no such dangers, for you, I am assured, are well advised. You do not stand alone. I who had barely known my mother, was ever encouraged by my gentle schoolmistresses to trust in the goodness of mankind. Unprepared was I for the way of the world. How might I have understood what I was to encounter, what treachery is there—that the fairest-spoken, engaging character may destroy—heartlessly, without a care."

Recovering herself and in some embarrassment, she turned to her son and added, "Yet I feel little remorse. Having once given my heart generously, I live for my child, and hope to see him to proper manhood."

Miss Dashwood made her adieus. As she hurried

back through the fading, cold light, she thought of her own sister, wronged by the very one who had caused this poor lady's ruin. Eliza Williams' fate oppressed her thoughts.

18

It had been previously fixed upon that Mr. du
Plessy would attend the ladies for the assembly to
be held at week's end. Margaret's anticipation of
the event was avid, as there had been some talk
concerning the introduction of an enchanting
dance newly brought from London. So much whispering had preceded its arrival that everyone had
naturally become impatient to see it performed.
And there could be little question that the whole
of fashionable Brighton must make its appearance
for this stylish diversion.

The dashingly uniformed gentleman appeared
his enthusiastic self, and more than punctilious in
his duties as escort. He was with his charges in
ample time, and willing to take them firmly under
his protection for the evening's festivities. Ever
courtly, he was, at the same moment, overpowered
by their coifs and attire—protesting that he found
particularly alluring Margaret's shining hair orna-

ment. Tonight especially his compliments to his friends flowed with a lively ease.

Miss Dashwood's own greeting had been polite, if less effusive than when last they met. She nodded appreciation, and promptly fell silent. Yet du Plessy observed no lack in her. Undaunted, he began happily and with his usual sportive manner to converse with Lady Clara.

"I have myself already had occasion to study this daring step. For it is, to be sure, all the fashion on the Continent, as my own dear mother might inform you were she here with us at this moment. 'How can you doubt,' she would certainly demand of you, 'that survival itself in good society *depends* upon the accomplished performance of the waltz?' Nor could you question her judgment upon such a matter, as it is ever sound. Ladies, this very evening, I shall be honored to show it you, that is, if the Brighton musicians are up to the task.''

The young man was as good as his word. When he saw that the dance was much favored in the programme by the artists in attendance at the hall, he immediately undertook to guide them in its intricacies. And to Margaret the very spectacle was dazzling. Indeed, to see two or three dozen couples, joined together like planet and satellite, spinning in whirls around the immense circle, each gentleman's right arm around the waist of his lady, while her left hand rested negligently on his shoulder. The vast ballroom buzzed with the sight of it!

And when after an extended trial in the company

of the beaming elder lady, the young officer offered his arm to Miss Dashwood, she was already
enticed, and must of course follow. Before she
knew it, they two were quite suddenly face to face,
in each other's arms, turning in giddy motion over
the great circle, and he the while fixing her with
his eyes.

The sureness of touch and the deftness with
which he led her directly into the rhythm (whispering that in each lunation they need make six
steps only, with the count swift), combined with
his delicate concern for her hesitations, encouraged his partner to a smooth performance of the
revolutions round the circle. Almost from the start,
Margaret found herself accommodating his bold
steps, while above them the candlelight blurred the
crystal of the chandeliers as they moved. The pair
hardly spoke, and during their gyrations he looked
upon her alone. With the reverberation of the spri-
tely music, it seemed that there could, at least at
this moment, be little to damp her felicity.

The room had grown crowded in the interim, its
noise deafening as the many dancers streamed in
concert past them. It was only well after their own
waltz was concluded, and as they threaded their
way back across the vast chamber, that such elation was diminished.

A mere momentary encounter it was, in which
du Plessy's attention was engaged by a young
woman who saluted him in French. His features
disclosed astonishment at the abruptness of her ap-

proach. Acknowledging his recognition of her person, he fairly muttered a greeting, and in his father's tongue. Yet he did not alter his pace or stop, but walked ahead with his partner. Margaret witnessed his brusqueness with dismay.

For the lady, she saw, was herself young, notably handsome, and with an elegance of costume that was striking. The soft crimson of her embroidered net gown was such as could only have been fashioned on the Continent. In her white, long-gloved hand she held a fan and fluttered it about her face. Her eyes had fastened upon the lieutenant as soon as she had seen him, and as she brushed by, she had added, *À bientôt.*''

It was nothing, to be sure; a chance meeting; only an ancient family connection perhaps; it could hardly signify. Yet as they continued in silence, what was clear to them both was that their own pleasure had been displaced. Glancing at the gentleman beside her, Margaret sensed his distraction; a morose expression shadowed the gentleman's features. Nor did he offer his companion further explanation.

But now they were rejoining Lady Clara, who had watched them with admiration as they waltzed, and he must rally. The lady had feasted on the sight and would herself offer some merriment in return for such a diverting performance.

''My dear Margaret, with what grace you have adapted to these lively steps! Ah, me, and how easily does dancing come to the young. Instead, the rest of us, feeling our mortal bones, must be dogged in the accomplishment of the same. I must suppose that youth in movement is its own glowing effect.''

With the hall filled to capacity by so many gentlemen, Miss Dashwood found herself much in request. She was claimed by an eager young man awaiting his dance. Fortunately, the orchestra commenced this time with a more stately exercise, a traditional longaways, and she set forth for it with him contentedly enough.

Lady Clara, left with the Mr. du Plessy, fell to surveying the glittering ballroom before them. It seemed to her that this evening's assembly presented a remarkably large assortment of French people.

''Surely you have observed it yourself, Sir,'' said she. ''Brighton's attractions have become something of a magnet for these Gallic hunters, horse racers, and coachers. For each day yet another 'Monsieur le duc,' or 'Madame la princesse,' as though by miracle, emerges from the sea. All these marquises, these counts, the very choicest members of society are arrived here with every tide, such is the welcoming aspect of our beloved watering-place. A fashionable tribe they are too; with their elegance, they add to all of the Brighton's gaiety.''

''You speak truly, Madam, in that many come. Yet what may appear to you merely an 'Anglomanie' that has swept French society and caused the well-born to abandon the artificial life of Paris *salons,* to change their lace ruffles and red-heeled shoes for plain cravats and riding boots—this is not whim alone. Where in better times these lords and ladies might have toured the Continent or arranged for their season at the theater, they now must sacrifice all, become fugitives that choose exile instead. Could I but tell you, dear Lady Clara, of their desperation, of the subterfuges they must employ to make the journey, it must surely appall you. Alas, whatever the carefree sophistication of the seaside and its revelers, abhor it or no, they *must* come if they value their lives, for such is the present chaos in their native land. A sad, sorry state for all of them, and for us as well, who are thus caught up in such struggle.''

Though du Plessy spoke earnestly, ever his courteous self, the lady could tell that his earlier ease, his open jocularity, was gone. His concentration was elsewhere, for as he spoke, he glanced across the room with some urgency. It was not long before he bowed to Lady Clara and asked to be excused.

As for Miss Dashwood, she had the meanwhile turned her own thoughts to the dance and her new companion. The evening must continue to delight, just as it had begun. As she danced, she made every effort to engage her partner, attempting one subject after another. But he was one whose shyness made any conversation an effort. So released from talking, she could not help observing, while progressing down the line, Mr. William du Plessy striding through the room towards the woman who had acknowledged his presence upon the dance floor.

There he stood in close converse with his friend. Margaret could hear nothing of the exchange, but whatever its matter, it was clearly of import, as she could discern by the lady's gestures and du Plessy's grave aspect.

When the officer returned to them, the evening proceeded as before; but without spirit. Miss Dashwood was distant, her reserve once more in evidence. As for Lady Clara, she was merely fatigued. And the gentleman himself was less than exuberant. It was only upon their arrival at their quarters, as he made his farewells—Lady Clara having hastened to retire—that he spoke.

"I have," began he, with eyes glowing, "intelligence of some urgency to convey, Miss Dashwood, but had no wish to spoil the evening for the telling of it. I have learned with regret that I must leave my good friends in Brighton; nor can I say when I shall be at liberty to reclaim them. How I should have wished to linger in your company…"

She heard with anxiety, but could only respond, "You, Sir, must of course attend to your allegiances. You need make no apology to me. Your acquaintances are many. *You* must to your friends, I to mine own. Do not err on my account. You need regret nothing. I expect little, nor do I await your attentions.''

Soon after, he was gone altogether. And there was an end to it.

Part Five

19

We have already been persuaded of Dr. Russell's wise dictum that the sea is a match for every disorder. Whether it be for the most serious of ailments, as of the lungs, the blood, or the stomach, or, when facing your minor complaints—the momentary want of spirit, of appetite, or even the loss of a cheerful humor—its healing powers have seldom proved less than miraculous.

Our determined heroine's full credence in this infallibility must certainly cure her of any regrets concerning her too cruel dismissal of William du Plessy in his late approach to her. Thus, within the next days she rallied and was sufficiently recovered at least to remind herself once more of the remarkable good fortune which had carried her to this splendid watering-place, with its diversions and delights.

True, that evening at the assembly in the company of the officer had been followed by silence from this young man. Then intelligence came of his departure from Brighton altogether. And more curious, even now his own regiment remained in place on the Downs. Only William du Plessy himself, together with a select number from the prince's own 14th Dragoons, had vanished of a sudden. None were to be seen at the seasonal enjoyments the ladies continued to frequent.

Not long thereafter, yet another turn of events overtook the attention of Miss Dashwood and of her good friend. In a visit to the Duke Street Theater in New Road, they discovered upon entering that a gentleman and lady had already taken their places in the very row in which they had reserved seats. It fell to Margaret to disturb the pair into rising, to allow them passage. Little doubt there could be of the gentleman's irritation at this inconvenience. It was only upon her turning towards them that she was startled to recognize her very own brother Mr. John Dashwood, with Fanny his wife. Seeing his youngest sister before him, that gentleman's demeanor altered appreciably. He was not only glad to find her, but expressed himself warmly to that effect, so energetically even that those surrounding them were given to understand just what a delightful coincidence had there occurred.

"Sweet child!" cried he, "I had no idea of *your* being in Brighton. Had I so much as a hint of your presence here, dear girl, I quite assure you I should have called upon you the instant following our arrival from Norland." Returning to his wife, "We, along with our dear Harry—for whose health's sake it is that we have come—have been at the seaside these many days, have we not, Fanny?''

Mrs. John Dashwood gazed now upon her sister and took her hand, though with considerably less enthusiasm than her husband. Studying the intruders, she seated herself again and rearranged her skirts. Only then did she deign to address her.

''I warrant, I should hardly have picked you out from among the many here attending. You are most certainly grown. Are you truly the same Margaret, that youngest and most awkward of all John's sisters, whom I remember from so long ago when you awaited our coming in that sadly neglected Norland we found upon your father's death?''

Then, as though in no genuine expectation of reply, she directed her stare promptly at Margaret's companion. She *was* curious to learn just who this distinguished figure could be. Her scrutiny might have been conducted through a spyglass, so intently did Mrs. Dashwood survey detail and gesture as Margaret presented her relatives to Lady Clara. Apparently, what she observed perplexed her the more. The lady's look, her dress, bespoke gentility. And when Margaret next explained to the pair that Lady Clara was longtime friend to Mrs. Jennings, and herself a widow, even the gentleman's interest was drawn. To John and Fanny Dashwood, these were immediate signs of potential. And what might serve their sister better? Surely, here was a creditable acquisition for this inept member of their family to have made. That their cupidity was aroused was perfectly evident, and with it came their genial approval.

"We have ourselves taken lodgings at the Lewes' Crescent in the Square," began John Dashwood grandly, "in order that nothing obstruct us from an open view of the sea. From our terrace we contemplate, for hours on end—" and he might have rhapsodized more, but for the orchestra's own fanfare.

Still he persisted, managing in a whisper to communicate his and his wife's eagerness to wait upon the ladies on the morrow. During the interval came even further efforts from a newly tantalized Mrs. John Dashwood towards the youngest of her husband's family.

"Dear Margaret," pronounced she then, "I have so often heard of your tender ministrations to the Middleton children. My compliments to you. When you come to reacquaint yourself with *our* fine boy—your very own nephew—perhaps you shall be equally anxious to see to *his* emergence. We would ever welcome you at Norland in the purpose."

Early the next day, the Dashwoods were true to their word. Appearing at Gardiner Street accompanied by their eight-year-old, they were much taken by the imposing quarters they entered. Lady Clara was her good, patient self, warm, though reserved in their company. She welcomed them, ushering them into the drawing room for refreshment.

Harry Dashwood had indeed grown tall. He stood straight, very like his father, and bore his aspect—a proper-looking lad already for his years. Any first determination might be much in his favor. Unfortunately, a closer view made visible as well an expression—some arrogance of the eye—which firmly reproduced his mother's own.

Yet his father's pride in his son was boundless. Today, he seemed particularly concerned that his hostess learn just how well the little man had taken to the rigors of the cold bath.

"None of those inland spas for the likes of our stalwart son and heir! You understand, we seek in our Harry the robust constitution; and thus have brought ourselves to this wholesome shore. Such is the demand of parenthood," declared he, "to instill discipline for health and happiness' sake. As one soon to be the head of our entire family, to command such enormous responsibilities, to be heir to your own dear father's estate—we must needs take steps for his sturdy development. And the colder the weather, as Dr. Russell insists, the better for the bather! It is the best way to cultivate in our Harry calmness of mind as well as perfect repose of the body. As for the blood—we must be altogether sure that it shall never, not in our dear son, fly to the head. Can you possibly imagine, sweet ladies, how bravely he has taken to the regimen!" Turning then to the child, "Have you not, dear boy?"

Young Dashwood was all too ready to oblige the company with a lively response. "Ah, yes, my special favorite in all of Brighton is the spectacle of the bathing machines on frosty mornings just at dawn. What a joy to watch all those glorious comings and goings right from the outlook of our own terrace. Though it is a bit of distance, that is no obstacle to me. With my spyglass in hand," added he, giggling behind his palm, "I daily survey the shivering bathers, gentlemen and ladies alike. How they do kick and flounder as they are doused by the dippers, and they so unattired. What a sight to behold! Why, if Papa did not insist that I must spend time with my studies, I should never leave off. It is a sport I could be at all the day long!"

A hush fell upon the room, but the child was so delighted with his tale that he went on unabashed, addressing himself to Lady Clara, "Best of all, Madam is how those bathing chariots do permit the most cunning of experiment. But the other day, in my own early submersion, I was able to try the truly natural effect of the sea upon a tom I had bagged to accompany me in this exercise. Well can I tell you, that for all of Papa's claims, the monster was not nearly so keen for Dr. Russell as we heartier souls. The little beast set up such a caterwauling the dippers would grab it up and let it free. In the meanwhile we did frolic, did we not, Papa!"

It would seem that Mr. Dashwood was not the least discomfited by his son's recital.

"Our Harry has, you see," confided his father, "something of the philosopher's curiosity. He would be turning cucumbers to sunbeams. The boy is forever preoccupied with his various animals, whether rodents in the field or our mice at home. An interest so profound, I consider we shall never talk him out of it. The other day, alas, it almost seemed as though Brighton would have been in hue

and cry over the fate of one stray cat. But then,"
he smiled, "there is nothing for it, we know that
boys must after all be themselves."

Struck by Harry Dashwood's proud disclosure,
and his father's approbation of such roguery, Margaret could only appeal to Lady Clara. She, for her
part, sat quietly as though hoping to conceal her
own chagrin. A relief to the entire company was
that Fanny Dashwood chose the moment to an-
nounce the latest news of the family.

"I trust, young lady, that you are privy to my
dear mother's ever-changeable heart as concerns
her heir," began she, her eyes sharp and full of
meaning. "Are we not ever so fortunate she has
discovered her error in good time? It is our hope
now that she must see the *proper* way for the family's good."

"Is she fixed upon a new course? And will she
now restore my brother Edward, her first good son,
to his rightful portion?"

At this Fanny Dashwood bridled. "Your brother?
Your brother, as you now think of him, was once
mine own. Alas, he has already moved so distant
from his good mother, and from us all, into a way
of life of which we cannot approve. We know him
not at all. What is heartening, and *should* be to your
sister Elinor and her husband, is that my mother
has now finally seen the habits of her second son
Robert, and especially of his wife, and acknowl-
edges their profligacy. Otherwise there is little, I
can confidently assert, that will stop Mr. and Mrs.

Robert Ferrars from bringing ruin upon the family.''

The lady then privileged them with a recital of Lucy Ferrars' faults. Only by diligent attentions herself and even, yes, flattery, had Fanny Dashwood been able to gain Lucy's confidence, and to learn the truth of their degeneracy, of the disastrous path down which Robert had been led. Having seen her duty, she was obliged to warn her deceived mother before it was too late.

''You have little idea, how could *you* know, of her guilty behavior, her want of concern for our family's welfare. Why, she has fashioned a Londoner out of our dear fellow! That is a condition I do not consider redeemable—surely the worst you can say of any man. I blush to think of my brother's most recent follies among those poseurs, dandies, and macaronis cutting a dash at White's. For along with these, Robert would gamble high stakes upon any gossip that comes their way. No matter if it be the outcome of the war and the fate of Bonaparte, or the number of gold icepails to be found at the pawnbroker's! They care but for the sport alone. Just the other day, Colonel Stanhope saw fit to engage my brother for one thousand guineas wagered upon the tyrant's being driven from Paris! Is there any fathoming such depravity? As for Lucy, she is herself enchanted by these capers. In her foolishness she reveals all to me. Is it not more than can be borne?''

Margaret knew not how to reply. She could only hope to assuage her.

"But dear lady, Elinor gives me assurance that your mother will be soon satisfied as to the fate of her family holdings. All shall be well since she has now the help and loyalty of your good cousin, George Osborne. He will guide her towards a wise solution to family cares, and you need have no more anxiety."

To this, Mrs. John Dashwood could only shrug. With the little patience left to her she declared, "My mother, Miss, may favor that young man, even to being taken in by his good offices, but you can be sure she would *never* entrust our family and fortune to one who has already reached the age of eight-and-twenty without having secured himself a wife. Depend upon it, my mother comprehends that the salvation of the Ferrars must rest with those who will have a care not to demean, but to preserve its line."

Silenced altogether, Margaret pondered how it might be that Fanny Dashwood's brother Edward stood so remarkably above the wiles and stratagems of a family such as his own.

20

Robert Ferrars and his lady passed the weeks intervening in high good spirits. Violent though his mother's outburst had been at Delaford Parsonage, neither her displeasure with his new involvements nor her rage at his London enterprise could daunt this debonair gentleman or alter in the slightest his present course.

How many times before in his years had he managed to arouse indignation in his splenetic parent? Since the death of his father, and that so long ago it was scarcely remembered, he had witnessed such drama, seen such scenes of distraction. Yet comfort there had always been, for Robert—endowed so especially with his mother's nature—understood her better than any.

He maintained a continuing, calm assurance in the knowledge that he could ever soothe *any* discontent, and that merely by his own person. His reliance upon such power over his mother was unshakable. Had he *not,* after all, succeeded in marrying his own dear Lucy—when the eldest of his family had been reviled for the same choice? And following hard upon, was he not triumphantly rewarded in the exchange with the precedence as heir to his father's wealth, over this same ineffectual and peevish brother? No, despite every difference with his doting mother—and the disquieting moments endured because of her ill-humor—Robert Ferrars fathomed her every nuance, and early comprehended the fact that *he* could do no wrong. Of all her offspring, he alone stood impeccable in her eyes.

Once he had ascertained that it was not in fact his brother who now presented danger to the security of his future life, he saw as being aimless his mission of reconciliation at the parsonage, and little need to prolong it. Not all the glory of Devonshire's seasonal environs could now provide more interest for himself and his wife. Thus it was not long before they too made their departure known to their bewildered relatives, and were off to worthier occupation.

Lucy Ferrars, for her part, had deemed bracing every thing they witnessed in the countryside. The very contemplation that *she* might have settled for such an establishment as she had seen in a community so insignificant as Delaford was to her altogether repugnant. In truth, there came new delight at the sagacity in her own choice: the stylish, the worldly brother, and a more consequential way of living. It was for her the moment to rejoice in her rescue.

Nor was Lucy ever without her resources, and in following their mother to London, she too was determined to be of particular use to Robert in ensuring the certainty of their retrieval of Mrs. Ferrars' good graces.

"Before very long, dear Robert," she declared, "your latest financial acquisitions alone will demonstrate to her just how remarkable has been our success amongst prominent Londoners. And then, husband, when you take your seat and make your voice heard in Parliament, she will once again be all affection, and your own loving Mama."

The pair were already comfortably settled in Little Ryder Street, just off St. James', readying themselves for a pleasant afternoon's excursion to a shop much favored by her husband—Gray's, in Sackville Street—when in the moment of their departure the servant announced a caller. It was Colonel Stanhope, a gentleman about town, whom they greeted warmly.

"Ferrars, good fellow!" began he in excitement, "I am most relieved to find you finally returned, and in such good time too. What luck for you that I thought to catch you up, to see you straightway to the Pugilistic Club. For there, this very day, Jem Belcher himself is challenged by Cribb—him we call the Black Diamond—that bout to be followed by Molineaux and Barclay—there is no telling which will possess the might and prowess to triumph. Every nobleman passionate over the sport—any gentleman of account—*must* make his appearance."

Robert, tantalized by this news, was loath to abandon his first intention, and he turned towards his wife. Mrs. Ferrars was, however, in command, and at her husband's service. She understood that *seeing* and *being seen* at such fashionable pastimes was of the essence.

"My dear Robert, you need have no thought of me," she offered. "Of course you must take up the Colonel's invitation. For myself, I am entirely dedicated to going in search of your Hatton's Lavender Water, just as we planned. It is, dear Colonel," she continued with an air, addressing their guest, "a scent my husband has taken a great fancy to. I do not doubt that you will be privy to its having become smart for every gentleman of substance since the Regent's own preference for it has become so much talked of."

Thus were Robert and the Colonel instantly off together to their pleasures at the club, while the lady attended dutifully to her husband's more pressing business.

Lucy Ferrars had dressed with care. In London, she knew, there could be no predicting the moment of chance which brought an encounter with the best of society. And it might be conceded that in her ermine tippet and fetching bonnet with its coquelicot ribbons, she did look enchanting. Better still, the ensemble was in keeping with *Le Beau Monde*'s latest recommendation.

Only upon crossing the square did she notice a gentleman approaching whose distinguished stature and dress engaged her attention. He too, it seemed, was making his way towards Gray's. They were nearly upon each another at the entrance before Lucy discovered him to be their newly reclaimed cousin, Mr. George Osborne.

Sufficiently disconcerted by this coincidence, both stopped, speechless at first. Mrs. Ferrars quite soon recovered her aplomb and addressed her cousin energetically.

"My dear Mr. Osborne, how delightful to find you again, and here in London. We had little leisure in the country to become acquainted, so it is altogether fine fortune that we may now renew the familiarity in London."

Mr. Osborne was openly astonished to find this lady returned so promptly, even unsure of what he felt. Yet he too, once looking upon the figure before him, attired and coiffed so alluringly, became more than receptive. The gentleman bowed and offered his arm.

Entering together, they found so many were there already awaiting attendants that Lucy would confide in a whisper, "It begins to seem, does it not, Cousin, that this afternoon the whole of London is assembled in but one shop!" As there was little to be done but wait, to pass the time the pair continued their converse for some minutes longer.

"And do you then, Sir, come to perform a commission for the benefit of some beautiful lady?" continued she in a coquette's voice. "How trusting must she be of your discrimination, to allow a gentleman to decide upon her jewels. I myself am far more fastidious than some I know of. I could never permit it, even for the most generous gifts. My own taste, I fear, dictates a greater dedication.''

"You do, Madam, give me credit for much more than I perform," protested he, "as I am merely the poor servant for your good Mother, whose own infirmity requires an emissary. I come to retrieve her ornaments newly repaired. My poor aunt is these days so in need. Her wants come first with me, as you know, and I have vowed to serve her while I may.''

"Ah, so that is your mission. I find entirely admirable, dear Mr. Osborne, your determination to make of us all your intimate family. It does do you credit," she said with a knowing look. "I for one welcome you as mine own, for I can see that we might understand one another, and could become friends.''

He stiffened at this, comprehending immediately her presumption, but, checking himself, asked, "Where then might be my good cousin Robert this afternoon?''

"My husband," said she gaily, "faithfully seeks out opportunity for the sake of his family in the company of those whose abilities are already tested. Here in London he solicits the best advice. We are fortunate in our friends and position.''

Having already heard expressed by the elder Mrs. Ferrars one fiery opinion regarding the value to his cousin of such commerce, Mr. Osborne might, upon hearing this from the younger, quite possibly have had his doubts. Still, he must concur with the lady. And besides, her charming defense of her wayward husband could only be admired, especially when conveyed by such eyes.

"What then, Madam," asked he, "might be your own purpose this day at Gray's? I should be honored to be of assistance, if you will allow it. It is the business of every bachelor to deal firmly with tradesmen," he laughed, "at least on behalf of a lady in need."

Lucy explained her errand, and though she had no need of succor, she welcomed him at her side. Adding with an air, "What can be purchased as far away as Brighton must be found easily enough here in the smartest of London establishments. Still, dear sir, if you insist."

Mr. Osborne's wish to remain in attendance was easily encouraged, and when her turn came to be waited upon, he followed close.

The meanwhile, Robert Ferrars, whose absence from the club had been noted, was himself being heartened by the warm welcome he received from his cronies. The occasion was festive, the assembly select; the cuisine excellent today, and the claret brought forward of the best.

To top it all, the matches aroused the fervor of the enthusiasts. Already a circle of spectators had formed around the first pair of boxers, and odds were being shouted back and forth through the room, while his own ally Colonel Stanhope presided over the betting.

Among the group was Captain Whitley, a patron of the ring and one of the liveliest of London's fashionable sportsmen. His rumblings were heard

with close attention by his intimates. It was clear to
Robert that only the most canny would seize the
moment and have profit of it. He would not be left
behind, and was among the first to place his wager,
with an insouciance that elicited admiration from
all.

"The day could not have been better," he afterward assured his friend Stanhope, "and the losses
be hanged."

Upon returning to his lodgings, a contented Ferrars found his wife chatting animatedly with his
deferential cousin, George Osborne.

"Ah," said he joining them, "pity you did not
come sooner, Osborne, I could have enlisted you in
the best sport you can have seen in years. Belcher
looked like a ferocious bull-dog in attack, fought a
pitched battle. It was a wonder to behold."

Osborne's own greeting to his cousin was
courtly. "Indeed," said he, "I would gladly accompany you, and soon. I too am avid in the cause,
especially when stakes are worthy and odds good.
Little leisure have I had of late."

"Glad to hear it. Now you are here, you shall
have sport another day, and the best of it! I confess,
I took you to share my mother's inflexibility; she
may seem to you unyielding in her aversion."

"Your mother is only unwell and, like women
of her age, dyspeptic," was his cousin's response.

"Ah, Lucy, you see, what have I been telling
you? Osborne too is here to recognize her irasci-
bility. I quite assure you, Sir, that whatever her displays, despite every show of force, my mother must

turn towards none but myself in the end. We need little worry that she must, and soon. When she learns of the imminence of a particular, delightful event,'' now inclining his head and smiling at his wife, ''her rage is certain to dissipate. An heir is all she awaits.''

His wife's blush confirmed his boast. George Osborne was silenced by this news. Declining refreshment, he explained that he had bethought himself of another, pressing engagement. And he took leave of them, going briskly on his way.

Part Six

Part Six

21

Love alone remains the happiest ground for any union. Yet when two people recollect—nay, when they cannot forget—a prior disappointment, and smart still over their first attraction having gone unrequited—what then provides safer structure than a match founded upon friendship and esteem?

In the Marianne Dashwood that was, we had seen the unrelenting pursuit of a cherished dream prove perilous. But in what followed thereafter—first, in abandonment of her hope of perfect attachment, and subsequently her acceptance of kindness and genuine devotion in its stead—how widely was that choice assumed to have been a mere second best! Poor creature that she was, what more could *she* lay claim to? The solution, patchwork though it seemed, provided her respite at the least.

Only consider the exact circumstance. Within this lady's experience, she was now able to benefit from a gradual revelation of admirable powers in her husband. Mrs. Brandon found herself departing from mere respect, recuperative though such a mild passion had proved for her, and warmed by a budding tenderness in which she was surprised to entertain ardent feelings for her beloved.

Her indebtedness for this realization arose from an improbable development. After Margaret's Brighton visit to Eliza Williams—at Marianne's own behest—her sister had written in praise of mother and child. Exclaiming not only upon "the beauty of the lad," but more particularly commending the uniqueness of his character, Margaret confessed that she "had never before—most certainly in those of my present acquaintance—encountered a boy so touched by natural grace. There is, dear Marianne, truly nothing wanting in the child."

Of the boy's mother, she wrote with sadness, discoursing upon a life so restricted and without prospect as it seemed for one yet young. "Still," she concluded, "Eliza Williams utters not so much as a complaint, and prefers to delight in the openness of her son's serene temperament."

Marianne greeted this communication with fascination, if with a touch of apprehensiveness as well. Many a time had she, in waking dreams, imagined the possibility for herself of such a wretched state. Even yet, there were mornings she rose in distress, unrecollecting of where she might be, and how secure. It came as true comfort to learn of Eliza Williams' sufficiency, her seeming content. Above all, it gave solace to know that she had survived romantic agony.

Even now Marianne could not but perceive the lady as inspirational. How often had she read in books of figures such as she—febrile, infatuated, wooed, and then, alas, forsaken? Here, for Mrs. Brandon, was dauntless courage in face of hapless circumstance. It could but remind her that despite every adversity, young Eliza Williams had been steadfast where she herself, in her own attachment those many years ago, had risked nothing.

Only some days later, upon learning—and this again from her younger sister—that the lady, accompanied by the boy, would soon be nearby Delaford for their annual visit to their friends the Edgertons, did she make a greater determination. She would prevail upon her husband to engage them at the House.

Colonel Brandon had not *ever* discussed with his wife his unfailing obligation to these descendants of his first love. This, in fear of giving her pain. Respectful of Marianne's fervid imagination, he had over the years used all discretion in his benevolent dealings on behalf of his ward and her child. Since his marriage, he had been unable to visit the pair as often as once he had, or to devote time to the boy's education and progress; yet he knew there was little to be done about it without the hazard of bringing the matter into the open, to the disquiet of his wife.

Thus alerted to their coming into the country, Marianne vowed to alter that situation. She would convince her husband of past anguish well forgotten. Let the subject be as delicate as it may, she could no longer remain silent.

"You may believe, dear Colonel," her protest began, "that in your ward's child I see nothing of my own life. *He* should not suffer further loss than already is his fate. Never because of me. I like yourself should be permitted to pay those respects due your unfortunate charges. I am quite able to welcome Mrs. Williams and her son. *Together* let us go to them at the Edgertons, and they shall come to us here at Delaford House."

Colonel Brandon was moved by such liberality as his wife now displayed; still he must hold back. "My own dearest, bravest Marianne," said he feeling more than he would allow, "you are too good. I keep my oath to my father's ward and to her offspring. It is my duty. But *you* bear no obligation in this, nor need concern yourself, now or ever. Sweet Marianne, I ask for nothing but patience for my effort. The child craves fatherly attention, a loving hand, and it falls to myself to see he is well attended. To bring them here to Delaford—that is more than I dare ask of you."

Yet such was her pleading and so genuine her desire to serve her husband, that at last he must agree. He would call upon the Williamses at Atherton Hall, and see to it the lad and his mother joined the Colonel at their estates for riding and hunting during their stay.

Soon after the newcomers' arrival therefore, the Edgertons brought their visitors to Delaford. Marianne, while greeting each of her guests warmly, was above everything eager to show herself un-moved. She chose for some minutes to talk ener-getically to the Edgertons of the remarkable prog-ress of improvements among the cottages that her visitors had admired as they traveled thither, while her husband led into the house both mother and son.

For what Marianne had seen before her, even *she* had not anticipated: the radiant resemblance in Eliza Williams' son to his father, John Willougby. And with what a fascination was she compelled to observe her husband's ease in conversing with this child, the joyful familiarity of his tone. Before long, Colonel Brandon proposed that they two should ride alone together that very afternoon.

The boy jumped with delight, chattering of it to his mother, "Did I not say, dearest Mama, that the good Colonel does not forget us! You see, he too thinks of our lessons in Brighton and remembers how well I loved the sport. Here in Devonshire we shall be free to ride like the wind, even to fly up after the birds if we choose."

And so did the pair promptly make their excuses to leave them, while Mrs. Brandon attended their guests. For the sake of the elder visitors, it was soon determined the group should undertake a mild stroll about Delaford gardens, for the sun was nowhere to be glimpsed and the day darkening. In this ex-ercise, Mr. and Mrs. Edgerton, assisted by their daughter, soon took their slower pace, and the lady of the house accompanied Mrs. Williams in their progress.

As they strode into the cold wind, Marianne studied the young woman beside her. Here was a face once luminous which today appeared faded altogether, and a form thin, subdued. She mused upon what beauty must once have been hers, and that not so long ago, for they two were almost of an age.

"I have so longed to see these grounds, Madam," began Mrs. Williams, excited, "they are, you see, the very trees and fields that my own poor mother knew when a girl growing up here. I myself remember her little and have but the sad retelling of her life to bring her back to me. Still, I have heard Miss Edgerton call her hearty, admire her pluck, and even at times depict her fiery nature in her youth."

"Of those earlier, innocent days, the Colonel speaks but little," responded Marianne. "Carefree I know them to have been for both your mother and my husband. She was indeed spirited, brave enough to seek happiness despite all uncertainties, as you yourself following her have been. And yet how wronged at the hands of the world…" She stopped aghast, fearing to have said too much.

"You are kind, dear Mrs. Brandon, but you err in your solicitude, towards myself at least. My own life, unlike my mother's is nothing brave. Foolishness, rather—a deluded girl's meandering in the realms of fantasy. Having entrusted myself once to a heart vacant of conscience or compunction, I was soon unable to find good in any about me. I could believe in nothing, *except* my own ruin. Yet," she added now with some emotion, "my salvation, my own revival of hope came in contemplating *your* remarkable husband. In this most superior of men—for there are few to touch him in constancy and valor—how might I not revive? Of all his sex, who can match your Colonel, without whose loyalty and devotion, there could be no life for myself or my son.''

They now saw before them the two riders—boy and man—as they approached, and Marianne could gaze upon her husband, so straight and fine, as he instructed his pupil. The child was listening in awe, eager for every hint, determined to please his patron. Brandon's disposition was one that seldom overflowed with jollity; today there was tenderness in his manner, gentleness in his hand, love in his eye. Before her was all that she had once yearned for in another. In her own gracious husband, she recognized a dashing figure.

And once their guests had departed, she embraced him and would persuade him of this belated perception. For the gentleman, his happiness at that moment was such as he had not felt, and he permitted himself the luxury of its expression. Might any knowing this pair in their earlier acquaintance have anticipated a union so perfect?

Unpredictable as well, if hardly so affecting, during that time was the alteration in fortune of the eldest of the Dashwood sisters. In her own quiet circumstance as wife to a country parson, Elinor Ferrars was astonished to find herself the most sought-for lady of their Devonshire countryside.

The change arrived almost unnoticed. Elinor's reserved husband, having himself once specifically renounced fortune as well as that prominence to be had only by the sacrifice of himself to satisfy his mother's family pride, was despite everything destined in his own passionate enterprise towards a measure of fame.

Edward Ferrars' exceptionality came to be remarked upon in Delaford, and the good parson continued to gain favor. With Gisborne, he comprehended that "a sermon which is above the capacity of the congregation to which it is addressed is useless." He resolved never to talk *beyond* his parishioners. His aim, unlike many another born to gentility, was to avoid scholastic niceties, the glitter of shining phrases, educated eloquence, lest he seem awed by his own arts. He even resisted the adoption of sing-song effusions, that affectation and intoning in the fashion of popular Evangelicals. No fine airs in his pulpit: simplicity alone should bring him the devotion of his flock.

To his admiring wife he explained, "I would be *of* them, not above them."

Best was his love for children, his genius for winning their friendship. By engaging Elinor to teach the more ambitious to read, and by opening his extensive library to those who could profit from it, he altered their world.

Elinor showed her mettle in that undertaking. Her education was equal to the task, and her manner gentle. The good lady's attentions were uncommonly encouraging to the timid.

"How enchanting to them seems even the simplest of tales," mused she to her husband. "And how might our parish be benefited, were we able to provide for them a schoolroom.''

It could be said that few communities in the vicinity were so well provided with either parson or patron. As for Edward Ferrars and his wife, they hardly needed to look back. After the tumultuous departure of his fretful parent, whose mind seemed ever more unsettled regarding the disposition of her fortune, whatever difficulties they must struggle against were securely diminished by the prosperity they found in their work. Thus, while the rest of his family readied to battle against a looming storm, Edward and Elinor felt safely anchored in the haven of greater enterprise.

22

⌖

Of a bright morning not so much as a week later, Margaret was busy dressing for a jaunt in the outdoors in company with her venturesome hostess, when there was a knock upon her door. It was their maid Sally, who brought word of a gentleman awaiting her below. In that moment, and despite every determination, Miss Dashwood started in hope. For ever since the abrupt disappearance of Mr. du Plessy—and probity itself enjoins us to confess it—pangs of remorse *had* welled up in her—and persistent they were—however resolved she had been to put him from her thoughts.

Might it then be he? After all, she reasoned brightly, her acquaintance in Brighton was with but few; who might particularly be seeking *her,* and not her distinguished friend? It was in such an expectation, therefore, that she took up the ticket presented by Sally, only to discover the name upon it was none other than that of Mr. George Osborne.

The young lady's surprise was prodigious. So

loath was she to admit disappointment, moreover, that she turned every curiosity towards the new arrival. Whatever could have carried *this* gentleman from his aunt? What might bring him thus precipitately to Brighton? His so sudden appearance cannot have been on *her* account. She was relieved by that much at least. Yet the idea of George Osborne here at the waterside was one not altogether lacking pleasure; and his having searched her out would certainly prove diverting. She hurried through her toilette that she might greet him the more promptly.

The visitor awaited her in the sitting room, and no sooner had she entered, when he rose impetuously and seemed almost to leap forward in greeting. Once again she felt his awkwardness as he stammered through an explanation that matters of business dictated his presence. More indistinguishable mutterings came from Mr. Osborne, yet his very seriousness, his confidential mein, his wildly uncomfortable gestures—all contradicted that claim. Surely, he managed to suggest, she herself must have fully foreseen, even anticipated his appearance at her door. He confessed that he had only barely stopped to secure his aunt's leave before departing London to seek her out.

"My dear Miss Dashwood," began he, "you will, I trust, remember that I made you a promise those weeks ago in Dorset. A word given is, upon my life, ever to be honored. I vowed then that I should call upon you as soon as I might—and with a prospect that it would bring us more pleasure than my previous attempt."

And thereupon the gentleman looked strangely oppressed, as if it pained him to proceed. "Might I also take the liberty to observe that you seem to have used your short time here exceeding well. As I gaze upon you"—and here his voice sank until it was hardly audible—"I observe that the sea air has improved what seemed unimprovable."

The fulsomeness of his effusion, the trepidation in his address—struck our heroine by its odd mingling of lively excitement and disquiet. If Margaret could be amused, she was nonetheless disconcerted by such a performance. She felt for poor Mr. Osborne, and yet would show him no sign. Such a pity did it seem that each attempt by this fastidious person to offer himself as courtly resulted in an enormous and somehow ridiculous effort. Behind his words must lie sincerest feeling, the best intention—how could there not? His utter absence of ease brought to mind that delineation by her beloved Cowper of one who must be regarded:

> *An honest man, close-buttoned to the chin,*
> *Broadcloth without, and a warm heart within.*

Immediately returning to him her gratitude, she began, "And you, Sir, are too generous. My excellent friend and companion here in Brighton fairly dotes on the open air; I merely profit from her great energy. But Mr. Osborne, my own admiration is the more profound for your independence, your carefree life. I will not deny that your calling here today all but astonishes me. How happily do you gentlemen assume your liberty: you come and go as you like!'' Only then did she allow herself to betray levity, adding, "But Sir, how cruel to have so deserted your needy aunt."

If she had meant to tease him into a smile, her gentle raillery was lost entirely upon the young man. He stood silent for a moment, crestfallen, only managing a disconsolate protest, "Ah, Miss Dashwood, can you really think that of me?" And yet rally he did. "I see, you will make sport. But I know you believe nothing of the kind—*you* understand that I do not, could never allow neglect of *her*. Since my own affairs are ever urgent in their want of attention, that most generous lady was content to allow me first to look to my business in London, you see, and then here in Brighton. I can tell you, however, I do have certain prospects, and they promise future ease." And smiling at last, he added, "Most delightful therefore was it to learn that you were staying here!"

The warmth of his address could no longer go unnoticed. Margaret, sensible of the blush that overspread her cheeks, bowed her head to await the moment when it might subside, and made no answer.

Mr. Osborne rose, and moved towards her with an importuning energy. He would have said more but for a knocking without, followed by the prompt entrance of Lady Clara attired in her pelisse and bonnet. She, informed by Sally only that her young friend was already dressed and descended, was surprised to find her in company.

The moment proved awkward. The room was

overtaken by a quiet that persisted until Margaret had composed herself sufficiently to present the gentleman. What good fortune that, as always, this lady's manners, the graceful tone of her welcome to the stranger, could restore them comfort.

"Dear Madam," he began, "you will, I trust, forgive this intrusion. I see you eager to take your excursion, and will not allow you to be delayed here only through my having called upon Miss Dashwood. I will, if I may, come again at a time that seems more convenient."

"Not at all, Sir," began she, unfastening her bonnet and outer garment, "I am honored to make your acquaintance. Miss Dashwood has spoken of her encounters with you in Dorset, and even of your many services to your aunt. And what can be more commendable, after all, than stout devotion to family?"

"Did she speak of *me?* I must wonder at that. Miss Dashwood has only now been upbraiding me for my slavish devotion to Mrs. Ferrars." Halting once more, he turned a satisfied glance at the young lady and continued, "But no, dear Madam, I do no more than that good lady deserves, so generously does she include me—and myself, orphaned so early—amongst her intimate family. Only when I can know her every want to be minutely attended do I venture from her, she who is as close to me as a mother."

The ladies sat with him some minutes longer, before it was fixed that he should return to dine with them next evening. Only then would they proceed with their day's outing, though they saw that the brilliant light of the wintry sun was already as high as it would be.

As the ladies strolled arm-in-arm upon the Steine, Lady Clara must express her astonishment at this visit.

"It seems you have gained in Mr. Osborne an admirer, my dear."

"Madam, if so, I can only wonder at it. I was quite dumbfounded by his coming. I assure you," she laughed, "there in Dorset his attentions to his aunt were as secure as here in limpet's to the sea wall—we exchanged scarcely a word during that time."

Lady Clara, considering their invitation to him for the morrow, offered a suggestion. "If you wish it," said she, "we might please the gentleman by asking Mr. and Mrs. Dashwood to join us at table. Is not your brother's wife kin to him?"

Margaret accepted her gracious proposal with pleasure. A note was dispatched to that pair, who responded promptly that they were delighted to be of their party.

When received the next evening by the two ladies, Mr. Osborne was decidedly more assured. Hardly discernible was any faltering in his speech. And yet surprising was the gentleman's reserve upon hearing from Lady Clara that she had added to their intimate group. True, he *had* had some word of his relatives' presence in Brighton, and most certainly intended to have paid a visit to them before departing.

As for enthusiasm, none was evident. Even so, once assembled, all proceeded happily enough. There was so much chat that before long both Lady Clara and Margaret found themselves somewhat disengaged, mere observers to family converse.

"And is my sweet mother in London still," Mrs. John Dashwood had asked, "there desperately awaiting your return? I myself have so often urged upon her that she come to us here and partake of the cure. But always she refuses *me*. Dear Mama, as you know, is much opposed to our newfangled fashion of sea bathing."

Mr. Osborne gave her every assurance of her mother's good health and comfort, asserting, "Competent attendants now see to her every need." He added, "I shall resolve my affairs here promptly, and be returned to her service before she has ever thought to complain."

The evening progressed admirably. Mr. Dashwood was after all happiest reviewing his boy's prodigies; his wife no better satisfied than to hear them recounted at length.

"We consider him so important to our future, we groom him as tenderly as royalty itself," concluded he with all the finality of a magistrate.

Mr. Osborne was of a sudden speechless, and stared at them fixedly.

Intervening to interrupt the lengthening silence, Lady Clara inquired if the gentleman enjoyed the theater.

"My time here is but brief, Madam, yet I shall count it one of my agreeable duties to escort Miss

Dashwood and yourself to a performance before departing Brighton.''

And to that proposal, the ladies assented gracefully.

In truth, Mr. Osborne's attentions to Margaret did not stop there. He returned every day for a week. And although she was constantly in company with her friend, he had determined to seize that moment when he might chance to find her alone. When he succeeded, he made his declaration.

How he proposed, Margaret could hardly recall, so unassuming was his profession of admiration. She knew not what to say. As for his urgent request to have her consent to speak to her mother, she could only demur—courtesy itself would demand it—and she begged his patience while she would think on it.

23

To have progressed in the space of so few months from unvarying neglect into the glittering realm of flattery, must bring elation to one so young. There are those for whom it might even have restored a confidence in the self. But to our Margaret, the surfeit of such sudden attention now brought but bafflement and dilemma. In this moment, not all her wit, alas, could serve her. As that third of a family in which, since the death of her father, there had been only ladies—and they given to presentiments—worse, forebodings—she found herself ensnared by those very sensations she had so often witnessed during the long years of their trials.

Despite every confidence in Lady Clara's superior friendship, she found herself longing yet for the sweet simplicity of their Devonshire cottage and her mother's comfort. It could not be charged that she was ungrateful for all that had been undertaken for her sake; in truth, she was heartened. Earlier, the very excitement of such regard having come so oddly in her direction had even brought her jubilation. For not one, but two gentlemen had looked upon her with some approval. Yet Margaret Dashwood felt herself all of a sudden averse to any disposition of her favors. She little understood this new turn to her feelings, and her own unpredictability came as a jolt.

In despair, she determined to unbosom herself to her kind friend, to give vent to her fears, to confess even to a sense of her own unworthiness. And indeed, when she began by revealing George Osborne's late proposal of marriage—so unexpected, so insubstantial that it seemed almost as if she had imagined hearing his words—Lady Clara greeted this news with some amazement.

"My, my," laughed Lady Clara, "that gentleman *is* in haste! Nor can I, my child, hardly imagine when he might have had occasion, for we are seldom apart. It would seem he must be entirely in your power."

Pausing then in wonder, "A man who sits so mute in company—one virtually wooden in the presence of ladies! This *is* a surprise. Only think what strong attachment, what fervor must be his, dear girl!"

Considering for another moment, she turned to Margaret with her tenderest assurances to conclude, "My child, he is of good family withal, a proper-enough gentleman. You ought not feel any disquiet. Perhaps what you need do instead is but cool his ardor. All will soon fall in place. And you may then begin to fathom your heart's true dictates."

Margaret, something calmed by this sensible appraisal and the solidity of such advice, thanked her friend. She could now put aside her chaotic thoughts, for the afternoon at least.

The recollection that they had appointed this day to make their excursion to Preston Road came as a happy release. She had so much wished for Lady Clara to know her friend Eliza Williams, who with her son were newly returned from their fortnight's stay at Delaford.

Mrs. Williams, along with her exquisite child, welcomed them warmly. After expressing her appreciation for the great honor of Her Ladyship's benevolence in calling upon her, their hostess turned towards Margaret, for she was impatient to bring her good words from her own family at Delaford.

"How delightful was it," she began, "finally to see the great house. Your sister, dear Miss Dashwood, is now the gracious mistress of that estate, and it has after so long become under her skillful hand the ideal home to Colonel Brandon that he so yearned for. And how generously did Mrs. Brandon look to our needs! Were we not well entertained, John?" she asked the boy.

Her son spoke up for the first time since their arrival, "Mrs. Brandon was kindness itself, and such a pretty lady she is, too! What fun we had! Such diversions as were there provided! The good Colonel's attentions were never ceasing. And later he would come fetch me at Atherton Hall and take me about with him. It is so fine to ride with the

Colonel, I can never get enough of it. One day, we rode after the harriers in a grand chase out into the wind and I galloped without a fear, did I not Mama! Another day, it was to watch the wherries race on the river. How vast was our time there. And best of everything, our visits to the stables to see the horses groomed and fed. There could be no better friends in the world than they. I for one would have none other.''

Smilingly, Mrs. Williams explained to her little one that if he found Mrs. Brandon beautiful, he must indeed now observe her very own sister who sat before him. The child went up shyly to Margaret and offered his hand. And when Lady Clara had engaged his attention in her gentle way, the two were soon chattering like old friends.

There came a soft knocking at the door. Mrs. Williams ushered in a gentlewoman who seemed her intimate.

''This is good fortune indeed,'' said she, ''for I shall have the opportunity to present to you, dear Lady Clara, my excellent neighbor Mrs. Powell, without whose constant friendship and assistance I should be much the poorer. Indeed, Miss Dashwood, I was most anxious that during your stay you too would come to know her,'' said their hostess as the visitor joined them.

Her guests remained with them a while longer, content to acquaint themselves better with this lady. They conversed amiably as young John sat playing with his new bilbocatch, a trifle Margaret had thought to provide for him.

Camilla Powell, though still youthful, was notably older than her friend. A widow, she too had been no stranger to adversity, having found herself in circumstances most unhappily reduced. For with the recent death of her husband had come the startling revelation from their solicitors of the failure of his numerous business ventures in Jamaica. Mrs. Powell discovered herself not only needy and sadly alone, but almost penniless.

Nor was the state of her health of the best, and it was to Brighton that she finally repaired, settling modestly as she could, in hopes of cure for her glandular ailment, before consideration of her future course or any return to London might be contemplated. To Mrs. Powell, her chance acquaintance with Eliza Williams and young John had been, she said, "Godsent, as I seldom dared venture very far from our own lodgings, in this season particularly, when the sun goes down so soon. It is dear Eliza who has brought Brighton alive to me. Reclusive we may be; but even so, together we are stronger, and freer to amble about."

Mrs. Powell turned her lively face to Lady Clara. They commenced with comparisons of their various exposure to Brighton's healing schemes; they numbered the variety of fashionable nostrums, and weighed their remedial powers. Both had undergone Dr. Awsiter's improvements upon the usual treatment.

"I too," said Mrs. Powell, "have profited by his mild method. There will ever be those of us, alas, whose constitutions prove too delicate for the cure.

I for one, struggle against the nausea, not to speak of a constant thirst from the salt drench. To be sure, the doctor's innovation of a mixture of hot milk into the sea water is salvation itself.''

For some while longer they assuaged themselves by the recital of their successes in enduring what only their natural fortitude could have achieved, until the light began to fade and the ladies made ready to depart.

. ''You must come to us soon, Mrs. Williams,'' offered Lady Clara as she stood, ''and when you do, Mrs. Powell may be willing to join you. Our own circle of friends, though not large, is most recently extended by the appearance of some of Margaret's own family—the John Dashwoods of Norland, and their son Harry.

''Moreover, just this week, we have been surprised by another acquaintance of Miss Dashwood, a cousin to her sister, Mr. George Osborne. The company could prove diverting, at least to ensure a happy interval and break the unrelenting round of our cures.''

To her surprise, this cordiality was met with an expression of distress. As Eliza thanked her friends, attending them down the narrow stairs, Lady Clara could not help but note, on glancing back, that Mrs. Powell had sunk to the sofa, looking pale.

24

The hall buzzed with theater-goers, all good humor and gaiety, while outside in New Road a throng of onlookers pressed to see what they might of so much elegance, for this was the evening when Elizabeth Inchbald would bring to Brighton her performance of *The Fair Penitent*. As to our attentive Mr. Osborne, all this stir in the street only denoted the need for extra care of his companions as he escorted them from their carriage through the unruly crowd towards the auditorium.

Inside, the ladies looked around with excitement, for it was whispered that the Prince himself might make an appearance. Certainly, this evening there was a grand presence of the military—the brilliant scarlet uniforms and the rich blue of the Prince's own regiment.

As they were guided to their box by Mr. Osborne's solicitous hand, Margaret chanced to notice quite near to them a party of dazzlingly attired ladies with their officers, engaged in converse as they too proceeded to their places. She started when she discerned that among this company was the long-absent Mr. du Plessy himself. And though she instantly turned her head away in embarrassment, it was too late, for he had already caught her gaze.

In a matter of moments, the gentleman had made his way towards them. Prompt enough was he with explanations. Over the last weeks, he had been occupied with urgent business at the behest of superiors, and for that purpose been dispatched to London. He had today returned to his regiment at Brighton, only to find himself enlisted in the service of his commander's entertainment for the evening. His unease at this moment belied that equable self they had come to know, for he stood before them solemn, saying too much—more surely, than was necessary.

Lady Clara, who knew nothing of what had passed between her friend and the officer those weeks ago, was unprepared to see him thus beset. Her own feelings of warmth towards him were altogether genuine; she was delighted to see him back. And turning to Margaret in the hope of evoking her enthusiasm as well, was yet again brought up short when she saw that her friend was herself looking shamefaced.

The good-natured lady could *but* continue in a playful vein, "My dear du Plessy, your desertion has been sorely noted. Miss Dashwood and I, though we do our utmost, hardly find our meanderings as instructive as once we did. You will, we are sure, be able to provide us with weighty protestations for your neglect," and here she looked upon his elegant friends, "lest we should think you have found yourself grander companions and quite abandoned us."

But it would not avail; the gentleman remained grave. He took no note of her pleasantry, murmuring again that there were few commitments that might keep him from them, that he considered their excursions his first desire, no less than his General's and his Sovereign's commands. His dejection was clearly not to be concealed. As for Miss Dashwood, she remained downcast.

Yet Lady Clara, endeavoring to deflect the gloom, now presented their estimable escort, Mr. George Osborne. Recovering his customary aplomb, the officer responded with interest that he believed he had heard this gentleman lately spoken of.

"Are you, Sir," suggested he, addressing Mr. Osborne with deference, "yourself associated with the military? Might I have heard your name from General Wellesley, my commander?"

"My various ventures here and abroad may have brought it to your attention," was Osborne's succinct reply.

"Or, perhaps then it is from London that my recollection comes. You will forgive my curiosity, Sir. What is it that might now bring you to Brighton?"

George Osborne, however, was not to be engaged by such particular notice. As he himself had never been associated with His Majesty's forces, it was unlikely it had been bruited in that quarter. Certainly, in the key harbors of the isle—where he regularly oversaw his imports of precious coral and pearl, it was possible that the name Osborne had become a familiarity.

"Are you unaware, good Sir," pronounced he, "of the paralysis in the commerce at the Port of London ever since the Customs House fire? Vessels unable to sail or put into the harbor, business at a standstill—all chaos.

"And can you comprehend," continuing with some heat, "the consequent injury to the mercantile world? It has been distressing in the utmost. Perhaps, Sir, though not immediately vital to the progress of His Majesty's forces, it is all the same disastrous for many loyal Englishmen." With this, Mr. Osborne led his charges away to their box.

The performance was commencing and the theater hushed in anticipation. Yet, it was some minutes before our heroine could still the beating of her heart, so flustered was she by their exchange. She had understood only little of the conversation of these two gentlemen; nevertheless, she felt herself oppressed by its tone.

As the orchestra struck up and Mrs. Inchbald made her dashing entrance amid deafening applause, Margaret calmed herself and gave her whole attention to that old favorite, Rowe's drama of woman betrayed. Here she might weep for the fair Calista.

When the actress cried out in heartbreaking tones,

> *Wherefore are we*
> *Born with high souls*
> *But assert ourselves,*

Margaret wished only to be swept up and carried away by the devotion of such a heroine, by her unwavering trust in her first love, by the poor lady's sad undoing at the hands of her treacherous Lothario, and even her end in dishonor and death.

This was not to be. Her concentration had deserted her, and Margaret Dashwood found herself continuing restless. Even the sweep of such tragedy could not now engage. She let her eyes wander over the center of the dark hall towards the officer's large group of companions, and was disquieted anew by the discovery of the young woman seated beside him. Was she not the very one Margaret had seen once before, and that on the evening of the Assembly Ball? It must surely be that very same, that stylish French lady, the elegant person she had herself encountered upon the dance floor.

Of a sudden the crowded auditorium seemed to Margaret insufferably hot. Like Calista's own cruel lover, she now thought, how fickle, how deceitful is human nature, its only concern for dalliance, and for pleasure in the moment. In truth, she wished she had never laid eyes upon William du Plessy here or anywhere else as well!

She felt herself dispirited, and her composure deserting her. She had been foolish, and vain. For after all, what could it matter to her just whom he might choose for his intimates? Holding back tears, she knew too that she must exert herself to retain her clarity even if the hope of calmness had forsaken her altogether.

Since the action of the play brought no relief, she fell instead to studying the gentleman to her right. It was as though she could see him anew. There between herself and Lady Clara this evening sat an ever-so-reliable Mr. Osborne, his head proud, his carriage erect, a man well content to be in their company.

The performance concluded, they moved towards the doors. Once again she glimpsed du Plessy approaching them with his group, and she felt the color drain from her cheeks. But Mr. Osborne, eager to be gone, guided the two of them forward without a delay.

Barely were they returned to Gardiner Street, Lady Clara excusing herself in fatigue, when Mr. Osborne could again plead in favor of his suit. A subdued Miss Dashwood now thanked him for his patience. She had indeed given it thought, she said. And yes, if he would have her still, she would be honored to become his wife.

The gentleman, greeting that acceptance with delight, now stammered to express what joy he felt, what good fortune was his, and what gratitude overcame him.

Immediately he would be off for London to obtain his aunt's blessing, and return directly to join her at Barton Cottage for her mother's own. There was no time to be lost, it seemed. George Osborne's determination could brook no delay and he was satisfied that none was to be anticipated from their good families. Nothing should prevent their wedding with dispatch.

Part Seven

25

Margaret Dashwood's late experience could but confirm the maxim—For those who feel, our world remains tragic; only for those who think can it still supply comedy. And even in so short a lifetime as hers, she had seen quite enough to convince her just how hazardous is any quest for the ideal. Better perhaps, she now thought, to applaud the realities.

Our good heroine, having chosen to make do, could yet imagine a patch ahead of grace, and hope of future laughter. Never mind a gnawing sense of lack, or her belief in what *ought* to be. She would finally accept that judgments based upon immediate sensation—fervor, partiality—can only distort; that candor was itself imprudence, and ill-advised. She was confident that in her acceptance of a solid man of affairs, all propriety and devotion to kin, all would be well.

And with morning, the sleeplessness of the long night she had passed in anxiety, her qualms began to seem but the timid caution of wariness, or a childish fear of alteration. Now Margaret was ready to reveal her decision to her trusted counselor.

She was at first checked by Lady Clara's expression of intelligence, even dismayed by a sigh she thought she had discerned, for her friend was surprised to hear of the affair's swift conclusion. Yet after some reflection, the lady returned a look which seemed not so much averse as it was something reserved.

Mr. George Osborne, she agreed, was certainly a man eager to serve a woman in want of a husband. "My child," was her word, "his determination to have you is there for all to see. Most remarkably, he asks nothing from you but yourself. Since it is my understanding that his position is secure, I can only think him proper. I trust you may come to love one another and find happiness together after a time."

"Lovely Lady Clara," smiled Margaret, "his very haste in the matter must speak for his attachment. I do confess, and wonder a little at it—he continues reticent, even tongue-tied in my presence, incapable of tender declaration."

"I myself," replied her playful friend, "always consider that it is far wiser for those who mean to marry that they do *not* come to understand one another excessively well, lest it impede their future happiness. Indeed," she persisted, "a long engagement is correctly reputed to cool ardor; worse, to replace it with quiet resignation."

For Mr. Osborne, immediate departure from Brighton meant that his business there must be arranged, and he set forth that morning to look to it. His errands, he explained, included interviews with officials and investors in his various enterprises. His new mood, moreover, suggested his prospects were such as to secure his future, and *that* he communicated by his demeanor. Not long after making his farewell to his betrothed, he was gone altogether.

So it was that Margaret must ready herself for her own leave-taking to return to Barton Cottage. And while she continued in her preparations, she recollected her promise to receive Eliza Williams and her good neighbor, Mrs. Powell, that very week.

Reminding Lady Clara of the engagement, she begged her friend to indulge her by honoring the invitation, despite her own need to depart.

"Such disappointment would be theirs, I know it, for the ladies have few diversions. I am sure it will please them to greet you here in these elegant quarters, despite my absence. Dear Lady Clara, can you explain how altered is my situation, my need to away, and make my excuses? When they learn of the happy circumstance, they will surely forgive me."

Lady Clara reassured her friend that their visitors would be well attended. "Sweet girl, *I* shall be the one sadly at a loss—with my good companion being gone—although I rejoice in your greater expectations." And the affectionate lady embraced her young friend.

"You, Lady Clara, who have given me direction when I was most in need, shall soon enjoy the happy effects. For it was by your good care that I have seen what propriety demands. And you shall be with us immediately we have settled—though even now I know hardly anything of where my future is. You must promise me that."

Their parting was fond, and Margaret could not but muse upon whether she might ever again feel such contentment as she had enjoyed in Brighton these weeks in the company of her friend.

Lady Clara's callers from across the city were expected the afternoon after Margaret had left for Barton Park. After settling them comfortably before the fire, she mentioned that, regretfully, the young lady was unable to greet them. Occupied however in admiring the grandeur of their hostess's well-appointed rooms and the light from the sea, Mrs. Williams and Mrs. Powell did not think at first to question Margaret's absence.

It was not until refreshments had been brought that young John Williams, addressing himself to the assortment of cakes before him, made the young lady their subject.

"Surely, Mama," he whispered, tugging at his mother's skirt, "Miss Dashwood will join us this afternoon?"

It was then that Lady Clara announced the news of Margaret's betrothal and of her swift departure for Devonshire. Both ladies expressed their joy, although its suddenness clearly had startled them.

"She gave us not the least hint of an attachment," marveled Eliza Williams. "Nor did she seem—as is lately the custom with young ladies in love—to be in the least preoccupied. How private after all is our Miss Dashwood! I hardly should have guessed—and she so open of temperament.''

"Ah, but you see, to tell it true," Lady Clara agreed, "it *was* something astonishing, even to the lady herself! Before she knew it, her young gentleman—a recent acquaintance—Mr. George Osborne—had sought her out in Brighton, intending to have her for wife. Upon my word, he could barely wait for opportunity to seek her hand!''

When Margaret's suitor was named, a profound silence fell upon the sitting-room. Mrs. Powell seemed once more stunned by its very mention. She glanced at Eliza as though seeking license to speak—but this lady was engaged that moment in explaining to the child that his favorite was going to be married.

Lady Clara meanwhile observed nothing of Mrs. Powell's distress, but continued with her amused recitation upon the singularity of the last days. "*Such* decisiveness, I do assure you, was to be seen on the part of the gentleman. But no matter that, after all. He is newly returned to his native land. Whatever impatience may be, if it comes from the desire to begin anew, to wed agreeably, to surround himself by family, it is hardly censurable. Miss Dashwood was won over altogether by such wishes.''

Attending her visitors more closely now, she solicited their own views. "Are these not commendable ambitions in a man? And you must know, his particular devotion to our Miss Dashwood must make him the more endearing.''

Unable to contain herself further, Mrs. Powell was moved to speech by this last. "Then Miss Dashwood has known the gentleman very little. And would she so rush into matrimony?'' Her face betrayed an unease as she glanced towards Mrs. Williams. "I fear I *must* open my heart, dear Eliza, before it is too late.''

"Have a care, good Mrs. Powell,'' cautioned Eliza, "I implore you. That youthful recklessness you saw in him may yet be tamed. Perhaps now he sets about to rectify all, to reverse every damage. All too ready are we to believe such young men irrecoverable.''

But Mrs. Powell could not be stayed. "Ah, trusting Eliza,'' said she, "could I but for a moment believe in his goodness, I should not...'' and turning to Lady Clara, she plunged directly into her tale.

"You see, Lady Clara, I might have enlightened Miss Dashwood regarding this young man's vaunting ambitions. Mr. George Osborne has been known to me these many years, for he was a devoted friend to my husband ever since their first encounter in the Indies.

"Well-intentioned he may be, or seem to be— and perhaps too fondly trusting are we, I own it— for we saw him as friend and mentor. And yet long have I waited to see the restoration of great losses. So long that I cannot but wonder what come of it.''

"Dear Madam, I do not understand you,'' said

Lady Clara in reply. "What injury can that young man have done you?"

She sat immobile as Mrs. Powell recounted her history. Her husband's ruin—even, it could be said, his unfortunate early death—must be laid to the delays, the disappointments, the disasters of such cunning schemes as were set out by Mr. Osborne. Their hopes of wealth had all but one consequence—her present impoverishment.

"Even yet, little can I fathom of his methods. Only the other day, this gentleman called upon me before leaving for London. In high spirits he was, for his prospects were once again of the best, though I must admit he never explained why they should be. I do believe he now means to salvage our former losses through a late and fortunate discovery. He is in line to inherit a considerable fortune. I have, you must understand, ever relied upon his given word, for my dear husband would allow neither thought nor doubt as to his probity. You see, Lady Clara, he believed in his genius; always arguing that before long his good Osborne would restore us not only what was lost, but return with a greater fortune into the bargain.

"To this hour, I wait that day. There have been so many miscalculations, and disillusions. Yet whatever he may himself hope to win, his want of caution ruins every attempt. I now fear not only for myself but for anyone who may be allied with him."

With what discomfort Lady Clara heard her disclosures can only be imagined. Before her, she saw a hapless woman. She could but wonder what fate might yet befall her own innocent Miss Dashwood in a marriage to one such as he. If only her friend were still at her side! Somehow, she must learn of the circumstance that threatened her.

Her visitors had barely left her, when she sat at her writing table to undertake the task. Even as she did, the servant announced the arrival of another caller, and Mr. du Plessy was already entering the room.

He stopped short, however, upon noticing the distraught expression on the face of this congenial lady. "I do beg your pardon, Lady Clara," said he, "but I see that I come at an inconvenient moment. You are in need of assistance. May I call your maid?"

Lady Clara said what she could to reassure him. In truth, she was comforted by his presence.

"No, do not upset yourself, good Sir. I am not ill. Rather it is that I have had distressing news which concerns our mutual friend, Miss Dashwood."

His alarm was instant and distinct. "She has not come to any harm? Dear lady, I saw her well but the other evening. What can be amiss?"

Lady Clara, reluctant to answer yet in need of counsel, elected to tell him what had been revealed to her within that hour. As she spoke of the young lady's decision to be married, and followed this with her late intelligence concerning the chosen gentleman, the officer listened in grim silence. But when she voiced her fears, adding that she was even now writing to inform Miss Dashwood the whole of it, he rose in agitation.

"Madam," said he, "there is no time to be lost. You must go to her at once. She must be alerted to the character of the man before it is too late."

Lady Clara sighed in despair. When she hesitated longer, du Plessy indicated that he was determined to put himself at her disposal in every way for the journey.

"I shall arrange to see you as far as Devonshire, for Miss Dashwood *must* be protected from such unscrupulous behavior."

As he pronounced these words, the grateful Lady Clara understood him. Though he would have her believe his concern for Margaret was no more than gallantry, what seemed obvious to her now was that William du Plessy was himself in love.

26

In her exhilaration over the prospect of recovering her youngest so soon, Mrs. Dashwood had advertised Margaret's return to their circle. Hardly were the poor girl's belongings set down in the cottage, when she was presented with a calendar of engagements already accepted by her loving mother to the Middletons, the Careys, the Whitakers. Once again, far too attended was Margaret's homecoming.

What Miss Dashwood sought, in truth, was solitude—the chance to reflect at leisure upon the promise of the future. Hers was the hope of an hour's contemplation, before confiding to her devoted parent the extravagance of her interlude at Brighton, and seeking her approval for the understanding she had there come to with Mr. George Osborne. Instead, she was once more drawn up into the meaningless, local whirl of Barton's routine sociality.

"Dearest Mama," she pleaded, "could we not contrive to spend our first evening at home? Need we positively present ourselves at the Park? The Middletons could, I trust spare us a day or even two.''

Mrs. Dashwood had however long since come to regard herself obliged to dance attendance upon her dear cousins' diversions.

''Would you then, daughter,'' began she, ''disappoint those who so await your coming, who think only of your pleasure? Our good Sir John informs me,'' she continued slyly, ''of his having secured for us the very horseman from Lincolnshire he has so often lauded, a Mr. Hugh Popham. You must know how insistent he has been to bring him to our notice.''

Inconvenient the evening might prove for the ladies, but go they must. It brought Margaret to see how little time there was to be lost. She *would* speak to her mother of the way things now stood with her, and caution her into holding back the news from the neighborhood until the gentleman had himself presented his suit.

It was an incredulous Mrs. Dashwood who gazed at her daughter and cried, ''Mr. Osborne? Do you mean that young man we have seen frequenting the company of Mrs. Ferrars, our dear Edward's mother? Can he be one and the same?''

To Margaret's asseveration, that it was most certainly he, she protested, ''But, child, I observed no special attention towards yourself when we all met at the ball at Delaford. Was he partial even then? I must own, darling girl, that to follow you thus to

Brighton is *something* extraordinary! This *is* a formidable conquest, I am willing to confess it!''

She knew her mother's propensity for the dramatic—the very thought of Osborne's pursuit could bring her to an image of heroism. "How little is to be discerned of a man's character at first encounter!" she marveled.

"Quite so, dearest Mama. An artist of genius may read a face, and take a lively likeness, yet fail to realize the sentiment within. But you shall soon judge, for he comes to us presently."

Little more was said before Sir John's carriage stood at their door, and mother and daughter proceeded to the Park where from the expression of Sir John the effects of Margaret's reappearance were little in doubt.

"Lovely girl," he exclaimed in greeting, "your weeks in Brighton could convince even me—a determined skeptic—that there *is* something to the talk of salt air improvement! He turned and whispered to the young man, "Did I not warn you!" before remembering to present his current discovery, Mr. Hugh Popham.

Margaret in her reserved mood only smiled as the ladies encircled her. Her preoccupation went unobserved by the company.

Seated at the elegant table beside a decorative, red-cheeked sportsman—the consistently silent Mr. Popham—Miss Dashwood continued reticent, venturing little after a desultory exchange with Lady Middleton concerning the perfection of her partridge. Fortunately she need speak only when addressed, since much was being made by Sir John of their day's hunt, and of the young gentleman's glorious horsemanship.

"Good Sir," began Sir John, addressing Popham, "if there be yet the fox born to outsmart the like of you, I have not encountered him. Ah, what could equal such sport! And the very best of it is, how little the business needs talk. I could not feel more spent had we rode to Bath and back within the day!"

That gentleman, grinning, offered after long consideration a judgment, "Sir John, if you do intend to tire a fox, you must expect to find yourself haggard into the bargain."

So did the evening progress—from the long gallop to its finish with prey gone to earth, their mounts blown and broken-winded, all spavined fetlocks and sunken croups—the finest proofs of splendid performance—its converse fixed obstinately upon the chase.

As they made their way from the evening's entertainment at the great house, the thought of her own fortuitous rescue from such tedium lifted Margaret's spirit. All at once she was happy. Even more, she reveled in her good mother's tactful omission of any hint of her news.

In the days that followed, Margaret found herself agreeably composed in anticipation of her suitor's arrival. Just as promised, the gentleman made his appearance; as for the business at hand, it was accomplished with his wonted dispatch. His greeting to herself was entirely cordial; his approach to her mother unexceptionable.

"Might I begin, dearest Madam, by explaining to you that from the earliest moment, I had favored your daughter as perfect complement to my new way of life. Convinced I was that she, she alone could bring to me stability, home, community. And you must be easy upon another score. I am aware of your family's reduced circumstances. A substantial sum as dower, dear Madam, means little to me, as such is daily to hand for the asking in my ventures. Capital comes as it goes. Such is of small consequence. Be assured instead, Mrs. Dashwood, my own view of matrimony holds its dedication for life's finer things. You have my word upon it. Your daughter is the very wife I now seek to secure my happiness. Will you offer us your blessing?"

How could she not? Satisfied, she applauded Margaret's clarity of judgment in choosing such a sensible gentleman. "You, child, have profited by example and learned much for one so young" was her compliment. "I cannot doubt that you shall be quite as comfortably situated as Marianne. My dear, I do wish you joy."

To his intended he had little more to say, and looked upon her with contentment, although not for long. Indeed his stay at Barton Cottage proved of the briefest, for the next morning he was making ready to depart—promising to return as soon as he might—as he was pressed by urgent business in the City.

Still, Mr. Osborne had not got quite away before

Sir John Middleton appeared at their door. He had observed a carriage by his cousins' gate and must discover its owner.

"Why, Sir John!" cried the proud lady of the house, "This is just as it should be, for you are to be the very first to know—if you can credit it. Here just now is our Mr. Osborne who has claimed the last of my daughters for his wife! He is shortly to become one of our own family!"

"Upon my soul," said he, "can this be?" turning to Margaret as if to scold her. "Sly child that you are!" And immediately his natural jocundity was recovered: he must embrace his favorite, and her mother too, expressing his pleasure.

Never before had this dear man made a visit to their cottage door without a cordial command that they dine at the Park, and today was to be no exception. "Good Sir," he exclaimed, exultant, "In celebration, you shall all come to us, and this evening. I commend you upon your choice of wife, Sir. Indeed, in our Miss Dashwood you have captured the affections of the most precious jewel in Devonshire."

George Osborne looked now upon his intended, and smiled. He could only lament how regrettable was his need to set out for London—to decline such hospitality!

Of the brevity of Mr. Osborne's current visit, Sir John was disbelieving, "But surely, Sir," he began, "you cannot so soon be torn from your enchanting lady?"

"Ah, Sir John," replied that gentleman solemnly, "our greatest desires stand too often at odds with more urgent pursuits. Still, you will acknowledge that true happiness depends upon the state of our fortunes, and therefore I must go. Be assured that once my affairs are secured—and that must be shortly—there will be every opportunity to take up hospitality in this beautiful country, and more, if you should see fit to ask again. Nothing, indeed nothing," and he turned now to include Margaret, "would prevent our acceptance of it."

Sir John, mollified by this prospect, acceded him temporary release. "To your business then, if it must be so—but for your pleasures hasten back to our Margaret, and to us all."

Nothing, signaled Mr. Osborne, could please him any better.

27

Hope is itself a species of happiness. It may even be the most gratifying susceptibility life admits. At least, for our Miss Dashwood in her present circumstance it must suffice. Once having given her promise, she could but go forward in confidence. It now seemed consequential that she make her decision known to the rest of her family, and she sat down to the task.

> *Dearest Sisters, I address you both together, as you see, that you may hear of the turn in my fortunes; that you may learn of the flurry which has accompanied a sudden courtship at Brighton, and be privy to my decision. Heretofore, the gentleman was known to you, I do believe, only as Mrs. Ferrars' nephew. Yes, it is Mr. George Osborne who has asked for my hand, and whose proposal I have now willingly accepted—just yesterday, with our Mama's blessings.*

*I know you will rejoice for me when you
have come to know all. Still, I should not be
surprised if you—Marianne—must be incredulous, and even cry out with astonishment at
my news! I do confess it, Sisters, where ladies
are concerned, Mr. Osborne may seem not of
the most sprightly and engaging. Yet I beg you,
do not judge his manner. I can esteem the gentleman; his heart appears true, and certainly
his wants clear...*

She left off, pensive, and scarcely taken up her
pen again, when her mother's touch was to be heard
at her door. Mrs. Dashwood entered the room exuberant, holding aloft the morning's post—a letter
from the eldest of the Dashwood sisters.

"Daughter," cried she, "you will be cheered to
learn of Elinor's latest projects. Such triumphs for
our Mrs. Edward Ferrars! Why, she is become a
godsend to the children of Delaford."

Margaret, always delighting in her mother's excess, especially when it pertained to the superlative
achievements of her daughters, laughed aloud.

"What more can the parson's wife, I wonder,
have succeeded at in their small congregation? We
know our indefatigable sister to be ingenious,
Mama; but—even so."

For a moment the lady sat luminous as she contemplated her eldest's undertaking—the education
of her husband's young charges, the relief of their
small discomforts—every caring effort on behalf of
his parishioners.

"And your sister remains assiduous in her search of a room. Until this, they had not so much as a proper establishment that could serve for their schooling! And now, imagine it, young lady, it is your own Mr. Osborne who has extended himself to serve her in that particular!"

Margaret heard her mother with amazement. Mr. Osborne, liberal in Elinor's cause? Was it conceivable? "But," she asked, "how could *he*, Mama, who has visited but once in Dorset, help our own brother and sister Ferrars?"

Mrs. Dashwood pointed directly to Elinor's own words, and read from her letter.

We could hardly have been surprised by any proposal more than his, so generous was it, for Mrs. Ferrars' nephew, George Osborne, his interest piqued by our community's woeful lack, gladly volunteered us his counsel. He explained that with the merest pittance for investment, we might garner such a return as would provide the very sums required in the construction of such an edifice.

Although in that moment, Edward could not yet envisage how such funds might be assembled, he was lately able to scrape together what he can. And now, with Mr. Osborne's gracious acceptance of these monies—even though they come in at so late an hour—we are happily assured that it will make the profitable difference we seek for our parish.

So we shall have our little structure after all,

*Mama, and in good time too! How heartened
are we by our good fortune. Oh, yes, and the
best of it is, as soon as your gracious son, the
Colonel, learned of the lucrative potential, he
too entered with us into the enterprise.*

Margaret found herself touched by this intelligence; it sustained her trust.

"Did I not forewarn you, child, of wonders?"
boasted her mother. "This is a financial scheme
framed by a man determined to woo his prospective
family! Yes, your Mr. Osborne *has* had you in mind
from the start. I do like him all the better for it."

On the morrow, when Margaret, as was her habit,
had gone off on her ramble into the cold countryside, Mrs. Dashwood was informed of a chaise-and-
four arrived at their doorstep. She found the equi-
page unfamiliar, the livery grander than any of their
acquaintance. The servant reported the carriage
newly come from Brighton; its occupants seemed
to be impatient, and eagerly awaiting an audience
with her daughter.

There could be no one more confounded than this
lady when she saw ushered into their sitting room
a travel-worn Lady Clara Ashburton, escorted by
Mr. William du Plessy.

The compliment of a visit from such guests was
not lost upon Mrs. Dashwood; she swiftly made
them comfortable.

"I see you wearied from your journey, Lady
Clara. Might you meanwhile not take some replen-
ishment, for my daughter is walking abroad at this

hour. Were I to part with you before her return, she should hardly forgive me. Do you then make for Sidmouth, perhaps, or Bath?'' she asked, assuming that her visitor was surely *en route,* and halted only for the pleasure of seeing her friend once more.

The lady appeared, however, to be preoccupied, and made no response to her offer of hospitality. Mrs. Dashwood, sensing that their visit was not casual as she had supposed saw she must not keep her guests waiting. Straight away she dispatched her man to seek out and retrieve her daughter, wherever she might have wandered—for in truth, Margaret's meanderings did sometimes run long.

Fortunately, Miss Dashwood was soon caught up and informed that she had visitors. To her questions, Carter offered little more than the news that a lady and young gentleman had come in search of her.

She could not imagine who might these callers be, or what had brought them. In haste, she flew home.

As she neared Barton Cottage, she recognized the carriage before it to be that of her dear friend— often enough had they two taken in it their excursions about Brighton. She rushed forward to learn what could have caused her to journey so unexpectedly to Dorset, entering the room with no thought to her own wind-blown state.

There was Lady Clara, and she embraced her warmly. Only then did she spy the officer where he stood apart. William du Plessy thus intimately attending her good friend here in Devonshire? And the pair of them so oddly arrived at her door? What could it mean? Our heroine cannot be faulted, if she found herself mute.

Were it not for the gentleman's intervention, the silence ensuing might have lingered. Certainly her mother was too intimidated to breach it. Du Plessy apprehended his traveling companion's wish for private speech with Miss Dashwood, which, with her mother in attendance, was not to be had.

Addressing his hostess, he said, "Your cottage is everything your daughter described to us at Brighton. Fine old possessions in these rustic rooms make handsome appointments. I have heard of your recent design to improve it the more. Might I trouble you for a glimpse of the results?

Mrs. Dashwood was relieved to lead him from the room to view her achievement.

"Forthright I know you to be," began Margaret immediately they were gone. "What can have happened of such weight as to detach you from your beloved Brighton? I charge you, do let me know what has upset you. From me you need conceal nothing."

Thus urged, Lady Clara spoke. "In truth, I hardly know where to begin, nor how may such an unaccountable business be broached. Indeed, child, what I have learned must come as a blow; yet I have thought and thought upon it, and cannot remain silent. You shall learn the whole of it."

Margaret listened as her friend unfolded Mrs. Powell's late confession. She told of her discontents, her suspicions, her fears for her welfare at the hands of her husband's trusted partner and long-time financial advisor, George Osborne.

Margaret hardly knew where to look, nor what to think. She struggled to contain herself.

"Recklessness of investments and coping with great losses? *He,* Mr. Osborne, so in need of capital that he must seek it from a widow? And flaunting his certain prospects of inheritance from his aunt?" Then, of a sudden recalling what she had but today learned from her sister Elinor—his solicitation of even *their* modest capital—resentment seethed in her.

"Lady Clara, there is more still," she managed, "for he has engaged to multiply as well the modest assets of my sister and brother, the Parson and Mrs. Ferrars!"

As her courage failed her, she resolved to maintain her composure. An exhausted Lady Clara expressed a wish to retire to a nearby inn. And with a promise to return the next day, she was escorted from the cottage by a downcast and silent du Plessy.

28

Wretchedness triumphed no sooner than they were gone. Only then did Margaret's relief come with her tears. How preposterous must seem now our heroine's search for sensible solution, how foolish her quest to live as best she could! Fruitless too had been every slavish attention to decorum! She comprehended of a sudden, that even had she given rein to the impulses of a wild heart, she could not have been more gullible.

Dashed, moreover, was all prospect of acceptance—even the illusion of possibility. What chagrin could be as bitter? She must acknowledge that despite stubborn effort, her emergence from uncertainty into independence, her pride in the sufficiency of self-command, she had failed to secure her future. In this neither good sense nor resignation had served her. Such ingenuousness as she was capable of! How could she have put faith in this gentleman? How accept from him empty promise without heeding the dictates of her heart?

Margaret, suspecting nothing, had conjured what she wished to see in Mr. Osborne—a person modest, benign, and so simple that he must be the partner she sought. As for doubt, when it came, she had chosen to ignore it, and deny true feeling. Her own acquiescence had promoted her predicament, and the recollection oppressed her.

She continued, immobile in despair. When later Mrs. Dashwood's anxious face called her back to herself, she was sobered enough to communicate her plight. Her tender mother took Margaret in her arms and held her. She, whose indulgence had luxuriated in the exercise of independence by her girls, who had rejoiced in their capacity to think for themselves, who had boasted that catching a husband was not what *her* daughters were raised to—that same parent sat anguished at her youngest's side.

Mrs. Dashwood hardly dared hazard words of consolation. "You do not reproach yourself, surely? This is disappointment, but disgrace, no! Your fault was trust alone, and I too with you. We were deluded. A scheming Mr. Osborne? How might we have entertained even the possibility?"

She sighed long. "If any one be humiliated, it is I, your simpleton mother, for having failed once again to protect her daughter from worldly treachery—and just to favor her foolish hopes."

Margaret looked into her mother's dear face and saw frank remorse. "Mama," she said embracing her again, and laughing through her tears, "had fate somehow allowed us to choose our forebears, I should have wished for *you,* and only you, over a thousand others.''

Both sat together quietly comforted by Mrs. Dashwood's proposal that they take some hot refreshment before retiring.

Even so, Margaret found her rest fitful, as she rehearsed Lady Clara's extraordinary disclosure. In her deliberations she could not but reflect upon the somber presence of Mr. du Plessy. How peculiar had been his appearance at Barton Cottage. Why had he come? And so dejected had been his bearing, hardly was he recognizable. Was it merely to support her friend on this difficult errand?

She found herself the more perturbed that he was privy to her mortification. To have accepted *that* man! What must he think of her now? Listless she remained, sleep having abandoned her. She now determined before all to address him directly when he appeared in the morning—to thank him for looking generously to her friend.

But when Lady Clara came the next day, she came alone. Since all her converse was occupied with her fears for Margaret's state of mind, that young lady was unable so much as to inquire after his whereabouts.

"How pale I find you, child," Lady Clara began. "I shudder to think that it is I who carried such ill-tidings. My night of sleeplessness must be nothing to your own distress."

She felt Miss Dashwood's suffering, and reflected, "Yet, having so improvidently learned Mrs. Powell's history, I could not rest until I had made you aware. Innocent Margaret, never could *you* be happy with a man of profligate ways, one so heedless of family and friends—how could you!

"I chide myself, sweet girl, for my own want of judgment. I, who have lived long, not to have sensed concealment, surmised deception! To have assumed honesty in ancestry, mistook respectability for sincerity. His good connections deceived me. My child, often are we so lulled by hope; we imagine too much.

"Do not despair, if this moment seems bleak. I myself am not unacquainted with what it is to have given love to someone unworthy. I do assure you that recovery will come, and swiftly. It is well he is found out before real harm was done you."

Margaret protested. "You must not, Lady Clara, fret on my account. Neither yourself nor my mother can be faulted. My present situation was born of foolhardiness—I do confess to envisioning that union in hopes of an agreeable future. That I have been duped, I must own, for Mr. Osborne's proposal owed more to his ambition to satisfy his aunt's requirement for her inheritance than any attraction to myself.

"As to the pangs of unanswered love..." Margaret stopped as she felt her temper rise. "Dear friend, when I think of his deviousness—and that is nothing to his brazen solicitation—how his desperation extended even to my good sister and brother's limited resource! I blame myself alone for my credulous reception of such a man's pledge."

Margaret's mention of Elinor and her husband

came as a reminder to the lady. "Ah, child," she interrupted, "Mr. du Plessy has already departed for London to right that wrong. When I told him of your family's investment in these schemes, he was in such a fury, he could contain his anger no more. There was no keeping him, he is gone to seek the villain out.

"You see, Margaret, there is much still to be revealed. It was during our journey from Brighton that Mr. du Plessy could enlighten me upon such improprieties as even we should never have dreamt of. Do you recall, for example, his speaking when last we encountered him at the seaside of a panic in London in consequence of some hoax? The daring escapade, I learned from him, was executed by a former Frenchman, one Charles de Berenger.

"But, Margaret, what our officer has since disclosed, is that his accomplice in this foul play was no other than the honorable George Osborne himself!"

Margaret sat stunned.

"As we traveled, I understood even more, though I could never draw from him such an acknowledgment. Young du Plessy has shown himself valiant in this and in every regard. His were rescues of scores of his father's countrymen and their possessions—those vestiges of ruined families—all the many gentlemen and ladies plucked from scorn and tyranny, and brought safe to England. They will forever be in his debt.

"Depend upon it, if anyone can, Mr. du Plessy will recover your sisters' monies. If this determination be at his General's command and in his duty, I know not; but I warrant you that for your sake alone the young man will hunt through all of London in pursuit of those ruffians, nor rest easy until they are run down.''

Upon hearing this from her friend, such a sensation of warmth stirred in Margaret, that it was impossible to remain collected.

Part Eight

29

Simple enough, given the inclinations of our good friends, should have been their progression towards felicity. When two people elect to take ardent notice of one another, to admire, and finally to love, surely, within a reasonable time, a prompt resolution can be confidently assumed.

Yet how difficult simplicity itself can prove! Consider Margaret Dashwood's rejection of William du Plessy. Upon what was it based? Her presumption of his duplicity. True, he was guilty of openness of character. His handsome face, his unguarded response to her every gesture had captivated her beyond sensible recovery. He had delighted her, flattered her; his encouragement of independence in her artistic endeavors had pleased her irresistibly. There had been no caution—no reserve in any behavior towards her. How might a young woman have been proof against such snares?

Even so, our Miss Dashwood had held firm—good sense, modesty, decorum all conspiring to warn her off. She had shown herself incapable of acknowledging that his offerings were from the heart, of comprehending that there before her was a man in earnest, and just as he appeared to be.

Perhaps our heroine's lack was in her want of faith, her jealous accusation and facile condemnation. And yet, how meager its source! Only Lady Clara's narrative of du Plessy's boldness, his perilous adventures in rescuing his former countrymen and bringing them to safe harbor in England, together with her account of those elegant ladies "who so hang upon him in gratitude for his valiant offices in their behalf," had shamed her from her anger. How could she so misconceive his character! In her predisposition to find fault, she had pronounced him unworthy without so much as a nod to his true nature.

Since she felt only perplexity, there could be little expectation of more from others. Her mother, told of Lady Clara's newest communication, was herself troubled.

"But Margaret, how might we have guessed it?—Mr. du Plessy already gone in pursuit to London? I *am* at a loss."

In truth, conjecture led nowhere. Only Lady Clara, once again her assured self had a notion. Before setting out again for Brighton, she whispered to Miss Dashwood, "I should not be surprised, Margaret, if before very long, there may come from all your trials something unlooked for."

Perspicacious readers are here depended upon. And if their engagement cannot approach such anguish as our heroine felt at this moment, we can yet aspire to engross them a while and ask their loyalty with promise of speedy reconciliation between our parties. Or if they should suppose the few pages yet unturned too scant to ensure the prospect of imminent harmony, then it is upon the proclivities of our favored muse alone that they must rely.

As to the occupants of Barton Cottage, they could now anticipate that any new tidings concerning the matter must come from du Plessy alone. And make his appearance in Devonshire he did in good time.

It was with some apprehensiveness that they greeted the gentleman. Margaret, still abject, could only depend upon her mother to address him.

"I considered it my duty," he solemnly announced, "to come to you at the earliest possible moment and report the result of my late mission in London."

The ladies listened as du Plessy recounted for them his uncovery, in the name of the Regent, of perpetrators of a fraud on the Stock Exchange—an event which so rocked London that there was panic in shipping and investment.

"You, Miss Dashwood, might yourself recall the urgency with which I quitted Brighton weeks ago, for it was then that my General dispatched me to investigate the incident.

"My father's tongue gained me admittance to the confidence of one Charles Random de Berenger— a refugee enlisted in one of our foreign regiments. What I learned of the scandal was that this Frenchman had devised an ingenious stratagem. And how simple it was! Clad in a gray great-coat over his scarlet uniform, he posted from Dover up to London, pretending to come from Calais. He bore news of a great victory over Bonaparte—and more—certain knowledge of the death of the tyrant. It was a bulletin sure to bring all of England to celebration; better yet, to set the market reeling.

"Berenger was even then eager to entice me into joining his select circle, for that, he swore, was but the start of the business. He boasted first of the brilliance of the influential associates he had assembled to carry the plot forward. Laughing, he insisted that his worthies were irreproachable. "'Good du Plessy,' was his urging, 'here is nothing but a prank that must fill our coffers and make us all rich—and lawful too!'

"Unfortunately my fellow officers and I—in the name of our sovereign—disagreed. We must see justice done. Berenger was, you understand, already in custody by the time I rejoined my regiment in Brighton. Only then did he reveal his prominent accomplices." Here he glanced fearfully at Margaret, reluctant to give pain. "Indeed, there had been talk of the 'fiscal wizardry' of one George Osborne. What should I think upon encountering him in Brighton in your company, Miss Dashwood!

"Further inquiry at the Encampment enlightened me soon enough. When I arrived soon at Gardiner Street, I was as yet uncertain of my actions; but upon hearing from Lady Clara of Mrs. Powell's undoing, my course was determined."

He paused, scarcely able to glance at the young lady.

"It was following my return to London that I was able to learn the whole truth of this affair. Berenger not only confessed the identities of his agents—he exposed their whereabouts. It was then that I found Mr. Osborne in his quarters, and confronted that gentleman. I can relieve you on one account at least, for I was able to intercept the post lately arrived from Mr. Edward Ferrars! Mrs. Dashwood," he concluded, "if others hoodwinked by that gentleman remain unfortunate, still, your own son and daughter are no longer in jeopardy."

Mrs. Dashwood thanked him, and thanked him yet again.

His duty done, the gentleman rose to take his leave, but Mrs. Dashwood was scarcely willing to permit this.

"Mr. du Plessy, you have served us as one of our own. How should I see you leave Barton thus, without insisting that you accept our hospitality. Stop with us a while to restore yourself, and partake of this afternoon's excellent hog's pudding and apple snow."

To this invitation, he bowed politely and made no objection.

As for Miss Dashwood, she understood of a sudden that she must now, if ever, rouse herself. As soon as her mother was gone from the room, she spoke of her own gratitude.

"Sir, I hardly know how to express our debt to you," she murmured. "Your exertions on behalf of my family are greater than we could dare have hoped. Your generosity is far more than we merit. This, after my so rude dismissal..." And she broke off.

There followed a quiet that seemed unbreachable. At last, the officer had had enough of it, and objected.

"I know not whether my King or my duty demanded it. But I must seek justice, and see you delivered of such roguery as this." He then continued in a more subdued tone, "Promptly Miss Dashwood, must I return to my Regiment, and soon to the Continent as well. I wonder if we shall meet again while our army is still at war."

She was moved, and started at this. The gentleman, interpreting the dismay in her expression no reserve might conceal, could remain silent no longer.

"I know you, Miss Dashwood, to speak as you feel, even upon a time brusquely. I have admired that spirited self in its lively response to adversity. Before I quit Devonshire altogether—who can say when to return—I must in truth know—even if not now, not yet—if *ever* you might deign to look with favor in my direction?"

Margaret could make no reply. To speak at all would divulge the ungovernable joy she felt rising in her. Still, there could be no holding back, not now, and her own fond inclination soon brought her courage to confess that *she* had long ago given him her whole heart.

Within the instant came the revival of this young

man's customary manner—the flow of such smooth words, as to reflect his euphoric state.

"My own Margaret! You *are* superb, even perfection itself! Your candor, your confidence, your splendid determination to live a full, a true life, despite hazards—to defy all disparity between what is, and what ought to be! And how I have admired and loved you for it!"

Our gentle readers may not wish to intrude further upon this most tender of moments, more than to take notice of Mrs. Dashwood's re-entrance to the sitting room, to discover this pair of young people transformed irrevocably. Only afterwards, as her daughter retreated from it that her beloved might present their case, did the lady comprehend the source of this alteration. And such fair disclosure as she now heard could only elicit from her—and this time with what a light heart—her joyful assent.

30

Could a circumstance prove more blissful for any mother? Not only had she seen her youngest escape the perfidy that threatened, but now this: the darling girl was ardently sought and won by her own preserver! In all of Devonshire, there might be encountered a no more complacent lady.

Such a turn of events, moreover, would by no means go long unnoticed. Sir John and his lady were first among the well-wishing intimates; and Mrs. Dashwood gratulated in their excess.

"Upon my soul," her neighbor exclaimed, "it does begin to seem like Miss Dashwood was heiress to the largest fortune in our county. Penniless she may be, but your young miss is capable of attaching every marriageable man in the kingdom! Yet, Madam," he continued good-naturedly, "I cannot but be amused by the caprice of the child. In these days, this is all the fashion, even is it attendant upon such remarkable charms as are your daughter's. One day she is to be off to comfort in Lincolnshire; another, her direction London's highest society; still another, is she set for foreign parts with our victorious army. So how might one such as I contest the whim of a lady who boasts an array of suitors as your delightful Margaret!''

Lady Middleton, kept current by her husband and her mother of each potential for the hand of her children's favorite, had been at first something surprised; yet she too was willing to advance her firm acceptance of Margaret's last choice. Said she, ''Army men, we are assured, prove gentlemen by rule, and they are *seldom* to be found at home.''

Hard upon that visit, came a procession of their good neighbors, to whom Sir John had promptly cried up the brilliance of this, *his* latest match.

As for Mrs. Jennings, her joy for ''her own dearest girl'' was effusive; and if she secretly fretted that the removal of the last of the Misses Dashwood reduced to meagerness their society during her long visits to Barton Park, she obligingly confided nothing of it.

Indeed, not long after, so it proved. With three comfortably established daughters, even their trustworthy companion was infrequently at their service. Mrs. Dashwood, though remaining domiciled at her residence, now improved by its broader stairway, was given to prolonged stays with her girls. Worse, so delicately was she attended while in their company, that when she did return to Devonshire, she welcomed less patiently the ever-increasing perfections of Lady Middleton's evenings.

Miss Dashwood's sisters' own jubilation upon learning how things stood was everything she might have hoped. Both basked in her prosperity; and were all gratitude for her Lieutenant's swiftness in extricating from the hands of George Osborne their lately dispatched letters of credit. And when soon enough they came to be presented to the gentleman himself—given his open countenance and winning manner—how could they fail to become his admirers and loving friends? Margaret had then written,

> *Dear Sisters, When last I did address you, it was with a momentous revelation—I blush now to remember it! Yet here am I once more offering extravagant news.*
>
> *Much is changed—altered so I know not where to begin the retelling of my fortunes. What more need I say, but that we must all learn how the heart has its reasons, even if at times we ourselves cannot find them reasonable!*
>
> *Before this, so unintelligible to me were my feelings, so wrong-headed my actions, so in check my emotions. Sweet sisters, I have*

*finally come to know myself, to see my way
again! And why? Well may you ask. I cannot
say, other than that love feeds the imagination—oddly, it makes us wiser, better, even
nobler. Dear Elinor, dear Marianne, I look
for your blessings.*

Scrupulosity alone commands recognition here
that Mrs. Brandon's response to this communication was unlike her elder sister's. If Elinor was
pleased, Marianne's fervor exceeded expectation.
Responded she,

*I savor your renewed faith, for love cannot
be ignored, Margaret, nor done without. I
can only wish for you and your du Plessy
that you may be as happy as am I with my
Colonel, who showed me its truest meaning.*

Not long thereafter, Marianne's elation was
completed in the birth of their first Brandon, al-
beit a girl. And though the child was at once
named for her sensible elder aunt, she was re-
peatedly assured of a romantic future by both her
parents—at least, once consciousness had allowed
her to glimpse the import of such wild promise.
Little Elinor was herself soon joined by a
cousin, one Brandon Ferrars; but this child's so-
lemnity, even in his infancy, portended a more

elevated destiny, a life in diplomacy, or perhaps even a mission to yet remoter shores.

Indeed, no limit there seemed to the bounty lavished upon the Dashwood sisters in those years at Delaford, and upon their families at large. Their good fortune extended to Edward's brother and sister, Robert and Lucy Ferrars. They too were able to reward their mother with a healthy grandson. Grievous was it, after so much vigorous enterprise upon the child's behalf from a diligent father, that there was in the end little left to sustain that prospective heir. Even to the elder Mrs. Ferrars, it finally came home that her dear Robert, in the very few years since his accession, had been industrious in emptying the coffers of what had once been ample family wealth.

That good lady's outrage over the feckless bankrupting of its assets went unassuaged. Alas, she never conceded her own culpability in that achievement. Having entrusted herself to the machinations of her profligate middle son, and later shown such regard for her nephew's business acumen that she too had made substantial investments under his supervision, she herself accomplished the destruction of her distinguished name.

As to the elegant Robert and his capable Lucy, they went on as well as they might in London amongst those gentlemen and ladies who loved them best, and who like them saw themselves significantly occupied with champion sport, privileged to be always at the center of fashion—and equal to any vexation that might inconvenience such enterprise.

Remarkably, Mr. George Osborne had himself escaped the fate of his more prominent French accomplice, eluding custody altogether. When he managed to raise the heavy fines imposed upon him, the Law proved lenient, and his case was not pressed. He was soon free to come and go as he liked. The greater tribulation arrived only with the disclosure that though he did retain his aunt's perfect confidence and the promise of inheritance, there was nothing more left to receive from her than that.

All hopes for a dramatic reversal were faded with Robert's heavy losses, and poor Mr. Osborne must abandon perforce his marital fancies. He repaired himself to his favored isle in the Indies, where such was his preoccupation with prodigious ventures that he was seldom seen again by his Ferrars cousins.

Especially hard taken by John and Fanny Dashwood were these disappointments, as suffered by their chosen heir. All dedication to his destined eminence was now as nothing. And who could calculate the further losses incurred by all those lordly improvements to Norland devoted exclusively to the provision of a proper seat for their own Harry.

Let it merely be appended, that when Margaret dutifully proposed to her mother that Mr. du Plessy be presented to her brother and his family, in a wish to acquaint him with the house where she had grown up, together with countryside through which she had wandered as a girl, her pleasure there was something thwarted—that estate scarcely resembled its former friendly self.

Surely nothing can prove of greater interest to lovers than their own very brief history, and they must needs recall their serendipitous meeting in Dorset, to rehearse each gesture and yet again each glance. Such recitals were now relished by Margaret: her William's first notice of her, his secret scrutiny as she sketched at Pocombe Bridge, his gentle urging of her diffident steps in the waltz.

They must debate as well their missteps. She *would* remind him, as he chafed, of that handsome woman who had boldly accosted him at the dance, whispering to him with all the intimacy of French manners. To this he protested only his innocent attention to his duty. And later, what else could he think: since his beloved had shown herself indifferent, he must cease to hope. When, weeks after, they had met again at the theater, her aloofness had confirmed his own hesitations and determined him to think of her no more.

How provident it was, they would marvel—and this more than once—that such an one as George

Osborne was elected to provide the means to their present happiness!

Mr. du Plessy, to the distress of his lady, must again soon to his engagement against the enemy. Fortunate was it that not too long after, the achievements of the British army resulted in the restoration of peace. The Regent, appreciating the gallant service of his regiment, bestowed a Royal honor upon the Dragoon Guards for their remarkable action in Spain. A hero of the realm, our distinguished young man's prospects flourished; he was in demand by his general, the soon-to-be Duke of Wellington. In consequence, he and his lady were called to London and often presented at Court.

Along with his bride, he settled for a time in Brighton while his posting continued at the Encampment. Soon enough, however, were they to establish themselves near her family in Dorset, and despite every exacting obligation, his place was as often as possible at Margaret's side.

While at the shore, she would have her husband acquainted with her Brighton friends, Mrs. Williams and Mrs. Powell, so grateful was she for their good offices. As for Eliza and her son, they were frequently welcomed at Delaford, for Marianne had come to regard young John Williams as an older brother to her little Elinor.

The widowed Mrs. Powell had recovered but a scant portion of her husband's means. It was

Colonel Brandon who undertook for her to restore a modest but regular income from what there was.

Lady Clara's lively countenance continued dear to them, too. And after their removal to Dorset, such welcome found she there that she was seldom long away from her young companions.

Whether oft-repeated visits by his formidable mother were as much anticipated, must continue doubtful. Madame la Comtesse du Plessy could, in truth, find her ease in London's best houses alone. Although Margaret made every effort, their own guests were not sufficiently elegant, and their ways often unequal to that great lady's expectation—excepting perhaps her son's associates who would journey down from St. James' for such occasions. And *never* could any have been supposed to approach those in her service amongst the Continental set.

As for our most radiant third of the sisters, her ruminations soon revealed that if experience—which the world commonly calls our *best* teacher—*had* led her astray in hasty rejection of a worthy hero, now at least it could serve excellently as excuse for a near disastrous misjudgment.

To sanction ideal attachment—to argue, in effect, for love, and love alone—may be ill-advised in this or any age. Yet when all is said, the inclinations of the heart *will* prevail, whatever the

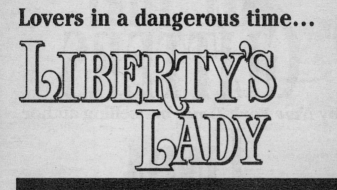

ALL THAT GLITTERS

by *New York Times* bestselling author

LINDA HOWARD

Greek billionaire Nikolas Constantinos was used to getting what he wanted—in business and in his personal life. Until he met Jessica Stanton. Love hadn't been part of his plan. But love was the one thing he couldn't control.

From *New York Times* bestselling author Linda Howard comes a sensual tale of business and pleasure—of a man who wants both and a woman who wants more.

MIRA BOOKS

Available in May 1998
at your favorite retail outlet.

MLH432

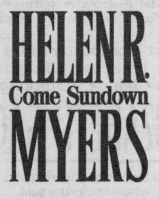

**Everybody in Parish, Mississippi, knows that
come sundown things change....**

Ben Rader was back in town, and, as chief of police, he
intended to use his power to investigate his friend's mysterious
death. He soon realized, though, that he was up against
blackmail, drugs, even murder. And his only key to the truth
was Eve Maitland, a woman he wasn't sure he could trust.

HELEN R.
Come Sundown
MYERS

consequences. And steadfast reader, what association for Margaret Dashwood could have been as exquisite as that which she presently contemplated?